THE INTERLOPER

BY
D. AILI

RIVER ROAD PRESS

Copyright © 1999 by D. Aili. Printed and bound in the United States of America. All rights reserved. First printing. No part of this book may be reprinted or reproduced in any manner without permission. River Road Press, P.O. Box 6857, Minneapolis, MN. 55406-6857.

ISBN 0-9671425-0-4

LCCN 99-93126

TABLE OF CONTENTS

Part One

I.	Koko	1
II.	Bandit	2
III.	The Meeting	5
IV.	Just a Glimpse	9
V.	The Year of the Wolf	11
VI.	The Dog-Lady	15
VII.	"Lucky"	18
VIII.	Away in a Manger	24
IX.	Trial by Ice	29
X.	A Legend in Her Own Time	36
XI.	To Catch a Wily Wolf	41
XII.	Winter Wonderland	46
XIII.	The Sunday Visit	53
XIV.	Build It, and She Will Come	57
XV.	The Clock is Ticking	62
XVI.	The Trap is Set	71
XVII.	The Trap is Sprung	78

TABLE OF CONTENTS

Part Two

XVIII.	The Cave	87
XIX.	Silent Night	94
XX.	The Appointment	100
XXI.	Hellhound	105
XXII.	The Return of Hellhound	111
XXIII.	"Blondie"	117
XXIV.	Just the Three Of Us	124
XXV.	Wild Kingdom	131
XXVI.	The Great Escape	139
XXVII.	Walking the Dog	144
XXVIII.	Romantic Interlude	151
XXIX.	Johnny Quest	157
XXX.	Our Door Is Always Open	164
XXXI.	The Turning Point	171
XXXII.	The Final Verse	176

To Leonard

In loving memory of Mr. B.

The Interloper

*Somewhere in the night
by the river of light
silent as a bird in flight
you came to me.*

*Somewhere in-between
real- life and a dream
where things aren't always what they seem
you came to me.*

*Your magnificence astounds me
(run, little wolf-dog, run)
Your history confounds me
(where in this world did you come from?)*

*I look into your wild eyes
I see the ancient fires
that burn you with untold desires
but you came to me.*

*Standing in the cold moonlight
senses tuned to flee or fight
if things were just so black and white
you came to me.*

*Your mystery surrounds me
(run, little wolf-dog run)
Your history still confounds me
(where in this world did you come from?)*

*Your wolf-mother I will be
someday I think you'll see
there's more to life than being free
you came to me.*

Run, little wolf-dog, run.

PART ONE

I.
Koko

Koko got up and stretched. The frozen January day was just beginning to dawn. The river below creaked and groaned. She arched her back and strained her neck, pointing her muzzle toward the heavens. Then she settled back.

From her perch, high up in the cliff, Koko owned a commanding view of the Mississippi River as it ran surreptitiously through Minneapolis and Saint Paul. She could see north to the Lake Street bridge, the Ford bridge lay to the south. Across the river, to the east, was Saint Paul. Above her, a good stone's throw away and guarded by a fence, was the picnic ground. It had been another long, cold and lonely night on the ledge she called home. Across the river, the sun was just beginning to peek through the trees. Koko waited in the gaining sun, her ears tipped to every breeze.

II.
Bandit

    Bandit and I hadn't been to the River at Thirty-sixth Street since before Christmas, as the weather had turned brutally cold that Christmas Eve, and remained so, unendingly. It was the tenth of January, the day before my birthday; I remember it well. The mercury was struggling into the single digits. After the sub-zero temps that had been, it was a welcome reprieve, and a trip to the river seemed appropriate. Bandit so loved to go to the river!

    It had been a rough winter for the old dog. He just couldn't handle the cold like he used to, though he still demanded to stay outside, where he would curl up in the straw bed beside his doghouse under the kitchen window, and wait for the distant winter sun to appear. But in these, the short, bleak days of January, it never came to him. The sun sat so low in the sky, and appeared so briefly, you wondered sometimes, why it bothered to come up at all. But his golden coat was thick and warm. (Though he barely tipped the scale at forty pounds, he looked to be more like sixty.) Curled up in his straw, nose tucked in tail, he seemed immune to the snapping cold and biting winter winds. Often times, as the winter sky released its load, I would look down at him through the kitchen window, and there he would be, curled up in his "triangle," three or four inches of freshly fallen snow piled undisturbed upon him, and I would laugh and shake my head. How I loved that stubborn old dog!

Bandit and I had been together for almost twelve years (and maybe seven times that, in doggie-years). For a substantial portion of my life he was there, steadfast, always beside me. Often, people are accused of viewing their pets as if they were their children, but Bandit was not that to me. He was my friend, my confidante, my companion, my alter-ego, at least my equal. Through all of life's upheavals, he was my constant, through thick and thin. Sometimes, he was *all* I had. We were kindred spirits. But he was a dog, and me, a person: I knew and appreciated that. But we were no less a team, and our relationship, no less vital. We shared food, played together, slept together—him usually on the floor at the foot of the bed. We spent hours walking the river together. We visited friends together. We were barely one without the other. We had a give and take common to any good relationship. I allowed him his weaknesses as a dog, and he allowed me mine, as a human. I knew his habits and inclinations as he knew mine. Daniel was convinced we could read each other's mind.

I realized just how much he meant to me the previous summer, when he suddenly became seriously ill, and I had to face the real prospect of losing him. And I tasted the grief that would be mine and glimpsed into that deep, dark chasm of despair. He was everything to me and there would never be one to take his place. I remember gazing at his doghouse, imagining the time to come when it would be empty forever. And the tears flooded my eyes, for Death was trying to claim him now.

And I remember, as he lay on the cement slab under the picnic table that summer, suffering in his stubborn and stoic fashion (his eyes barely seeing me, his body wracked with fever, his nose hot and dry), I would hold his head in my lap and drip water to him from my fingertips and whisper, "It's okay Bandit, if it hurts too much, you can go. I will understand," though it killed me to say these words and I knew that nothing would ever be the same again. But his suffering was great. Then one day, he began to get better, though he would never regain his youthful vigor. As Daniel put it, he had definitely "lost a step." And so I began to mourn his loss. The time had sped away so quickly.

And now, as I watched him get up, a little stiff in the right haunch, I could no longer deny the inevitable: Bandit was getting old. His ears still stood up straight and his tail curled over his back (though not quite as tightly), but his dark eyelashes had gone white, as had most of his whiskers, making his already white face seem even more-so. His eyes were dark and gentle, gleeful, though a certain tiredness often appeared around the edges. How often lately at night, I would look into those eyes, tears brimming from my own, and whisper to him, "Oh, Bandit. What will I ever do without you?" as I stroked his ears just the way he liked. He would raise his head and wonder briefly at the tears, then snuggle in a little deeper and sink back into sleep, to dream the dreams that dogs dream, and humans can only wonder about.

III.
The Meeting

"Hey, Bandit!" I went outside to roust him from his straw. "Wanna go for a walk?" Although the *w*-word had barely crossed my lips, Bandit exploded. He leapt up as if shot from a cannon, barking and dancing about, much belying his eleven-plus years. Bandit lived to walk. The walk-ritual had remained pretty much the same over the years: for sure, once in the morning and once in the evening, and then, since I wasn't working and weather permitting, a "bonus" walk in the middle of the day. I would wrestle the excited and squirming Bandit into his harness, grab the leash, and away we'd go.

On this particular day, Daniel (my long-enduring significant other) was sleeping off a trip to the east coast. He was the one who had brought Bandit home to me when Bandit was no bigger than a fist. Daniel was now a professional driver, and often gone for several days at a time. I tried to quiet Bandit, so as not to wake Daniel (which was no easy task), and hustled him toward the car. Today we would be driving to the river. Although in his younger days, Bandit would gladly and deliciously run for miles beside the bike, now the several blocks to Thirty-sixth Street could prove quite a trek for the old guy, especially during the winter months, with the deep snow and often icy sidewalks.

The place I refer to simply as "Thirty-sixth Street" is actually where Thirty-sixth Street ends and meets West River Road, the parkway that runs along the river, twisting and winding its way through South Minneapolis. Here, there is a small parking circle. A steep slope drops down from the parking area to a valley, which leads to another hill that takes you up to a clearing, where several unfrequented picnic tables and cookers stand. Once there, you are on top of the river gorge, with a view to the vista of the Mississippi River below. There are paths to travel, woods to walk in, and cliffs to climb. It is one of the many places in the city along the river where a dog can run free (as should be), and a person can walk in relative peace and contemplation. It is a common place for dogs and their humans, but on a day such as this, few would be out.

As we approached Thirty-sixth Street, Bandit danced anxiously in the back seat. His excitement could no longer be contained as I pulled in to park the car. He squeezed behind the seat and out the car door as soon as it cracked open. His nose immediately went to work, checking the "messages" from dogs that had passed, and of course, leaving a few of his own. Half-sliding, half-walking, down the hill we went. Though the snow was deep, there had been sufficient foot traffic here to afford some well-trodden, easily negotiable paths. As we climbed the next rise, the frozen river below came into full view.

Walking the edge of the hill, lost in thought, I turned now and again to check Bandit's progress. He was very busy with some scent he had detected deep in the snow, pulling his head out now and then to check my progress, snuffling and snorting, the snow covering his face, with only his dark eyes grinning out at me.

"Come on, Bandit!" I urged, and trudged on. When I turned again, the sight I saw stopped me dead in my tracks and made my breath catch on the intake. For there, stalking no more than ten or twelve feet behind Bandit, was a grayish, ghostly, four-legged creature, who seemed to have appeared out of nowhere. My heart cried Wolf!, but my reasoned-head countered with, No! It can't be . . . could it?

"Bandit!" I called, with a touch of urgency in my voice. "Here! Come!" It never failed. As soon as I tried to assert my alpha-status and command him to something, his natural belligerence would cause him to stop and stare blankly at me, dumbfounded as to what my request could possibly mean. Then he noticed the animal behind him.

Bandit turned abruptly and immediately adopted his Yeah! I'm bad! stance: chest puffed out, head erect and tail curled tightly over his back. I stood helplessly, twenty paces ahead, imagining the blood and fur flying, wondering how far to the nearest vet. He may have been a lot of things, but Bandit was definitely no fighter. As he stiffly approached the crouching animal, the wolf/dog suddenly dropped into what would be called a play-bow: front legs outstretched, rump in the air, tail wagging. The tension broke immediately and my breath released into a frosty cloud. I laughed. Just some old stray, I thought.

"Hey!" I said. "Where did you come from?" The wolf/dog, though obviously taken with Bandit, eyed me suspiciously, and stayed ever just an-inch-over-an-arm's-length away. She jumped and romped around Bandit, trying to coerce him to play. But after the initial sniffing and greeting, Bandit was back to business. He had smells to smell and messages to leave. The wolf/dog continued on with us, unperturbed by Bandit's indifference, content just to follow along.

She was a sight to behold as she bounded along. Her silvery body was long and lithe. She was all colors of gray and black. Her sides, belly, and long, sinewy legs were near white. The grays and blacks formed the appearance of a saddle on her back. Her bushy tail, tipped also with black, hung long and low. She wore a white bib on her throat, and what can best be described as a Batman mask on her head. Her ears stood tall and erect. The darkest hairs on her face patterned into a diamond shape, which traveled from forehead to snout, leaving her with a ring around each eye, of a lighter shade, that also formed the appearance of eyebrows, which had a rather comical effect, as they moved and cocked with each expression. She wore no collar or tags.

"Come here, dog!" I called and clucked, but it was obvious the animal had no intention of submitting to my outstretched hand. "All right, then," I said, "so, be that way!" We continued along down the far side of the hill and came back through the valley, completing our circle. As we began our final ascent up the hill to the car, I glanced back, fully expecting to see the stray still tagging along behind. But she wasn't. Rather, she had plopped herself down in the snow under a big, gnarly oak at the bottom of the second hill, and was gnawing intently on a good-sized limb that had fallen there. It was as if to say, this is as far as I go! She was completely unimpressed by our departure, and in fact, appeared quite content. "See ya, dog!" I called back to her.

I puzzled the short ride home, a little perplexed at the thought of an animal being lost and alone and in such a hostile climate. It was only in the 'teens, and the temperature was sure to drop well below zero overnight. But Bandit was happy and spent. Neither one of us could have guessed, just how often we would be back to that place on the hill that winter, nor the full implications of that first by-chance meeting.

IV.
Just a Glimpse

"I just saw a wolf at the river!" I told Daniel upon my return. He was up and on his second cup of coffee. Then I corrected myself. "Well, it sure looked like a wolf," I said. Daniel was more than willing to believe my first assertion, always ready for a new adventure. So I continued. I told him how she had mysteriously appeared, followed with us, and then stayed behind, concluding that she must be hungry and that I was fairly confident she would still be there on the hill. I could tell that Daniel was intrigued. "Let's bring her some food," I suggested. I was anxious for him to see her. He agreed. We shared equally in our eagerness and enthusiasm for any new or unusual exploit. But neither one of us could have possibly known where this simple goodwill gesture would lead.

First, what to put the food in. I had inherited several loaf pans from someone, which were truly expendable, as I had never baked a loaf of bread in my life. We filled one with some good, dry crunch and hopped into the car, this time leaving Bandit behind. (I thought the hills at Thirty-sixth Street would be too much for him to navigate twice in one day.) We parked the car and trekked up to the picnic area.

There was no sign of the wolf/dog anywhere, although we did cross paths with one cross-country skier, and a black lab, with person in tow. We decided to place the food somewhere inconspicuous, hoping the nose of a hungry pup would discover the meal. As I stumbled and slid halfway down the untrodden side of the hill, to place the food under the sheltering boughs of a tall pine, my eyes scanned the bottomland. There below, close to the river's edge, I caught sight of two parka-clad individuals accompanied by a large malamute. And then I saw her. She was gliding along the tree line, paralleling the hikers and dog. I fumbled back up the hill, calling to Daniel and pointing, "There she is! There she is! Down below!" He looked in the direction of my point, and caught the most fleeting glimpse of her. Then she was gone.

We left feeling satisfied, but not fulfilled. Although I was glad to have him see her at all, for had he not, I might have questioned the solidity of my own apparition. We spent the remainder of the day in normal wintertime pursuits, napping and watching tv, giving little more thought to the animal on the hill. As night fell, so did the temperature.

V.
The Year of the Wolf

It was about seven-thirty and twelve-below when I woke up the next morning. The sky was still dark. These were the shortest days of the year. Winter was at its cruelest and most unrelenting. But today it was my birthday, and a reason for us to celebrate. I felt the specialness of the day as I got up and started the coffee to brew. Even though I was well beyond it, I always felt a little bit like the kid on my birthday. In the bleak and pale days of January, it provided a glimmer of hope for the future. It was a time to take stock of the present, and glance at the past. But most of all, it was a reason to get out of the cave.

I always looked at the days of winter in terms of the temperature, because I knew, before I had downed my second cup of coffee, Bandit would be staring up at me with eager eyes, and then would ensue his incessant and insistent barking, hurry up! hurry up!, as I donned layer upon layer of clothing and laced up my boots, we would be heading out into the elements, whatever they might be. And though begrudgingly I might walk out the door, I usually returned feeling refreshed and invigorated, and somehow more connected to the day. Daniel was up before the coffee had finished brewing. "Happy birthday!" he called out, on his way to the kitchen.

We drank our coffee and watched the morning news show, trying to decide what to do with the day. We both agreed, it should definitely be something *indoors*. By then, Bandit was winding up, and the matter at hand was to take care of him. I hesitated to take him on the neighborhood streets: with the bitter cold temperatures, and the salt and chemical spewed streets, he was sure to go lame. He would need his boots. But trying to put boots on him, with him all barking and squirming about, was a battle I just didn't want to fight this morning. It was easier just to warm up the car and haul him over to Thirty-sixth Street, where he wouldn't need his boots, and he didn't have to drag me around on the end of a leash. I suppose I was half hoping to run into the stray again, though I really didn't expect her to still be there. We bundled up and left. Bandit was jubilant.

Bandit raced ahead and was up the second hill before we were down the first. We scrambled to keep up. As we crested the rise, I could see Bandit up ahead. And there she was, bouncing and frolicking and running circles around the perplexed Bandit. It was a delight to see her again. As we approached, her mood became suspicious. She watched us intently, with wary eyes.

"It's okay, girl," I told her, "we mean you no harm." By my tone, I think she relaxed a little and she became playful again—but she wouldn't come near us. Soon, another dog and its owner appeared on the scene. The dog's name, we would later learn, was Clancy. He was a white and gray poodle-terrier mix, with proper plaid coat and boots. The stray seemed to recognize him, and they began to play (Bandit was off on other business). Clancy's person, a tall man in his thirties, conveyed to us, appearing somewhat disgruntled, the fact that this stray had been hanging around here for quite some time. "Clancy!" he called, "come!" And then, "Cla-a-a-a-a-ancy. . . ." They continued on their route. The wayward pup must have thought Clancy better sport than Bandit, for she disappeared down the trail after them. We continued on our path, then headed home.

Once there, we again kicked around ideas as to what to do with the day. "We should bring her some food," I said. Daniel was willing. This time, we put some canned food in with the crunch, hoping she would be there to eat the meal before it froze. We returned to the hill again, leaving Bandit behind, but there was no sign of her.

"Maybe she's traveled down toward the Lake Street bridge," Daniel offered, "let's drive down that way." As we walked back to the car, we decided on a trip to the Mall of America, touted as the largest indoor shopping arena in the country. I could pick out some birthday presents there, and it was only a few minutes drive. It had been open for some time now, and we still had not made our first pilgrimage. We just weren't the mall-going type. But it was something new and different to do for my birthday, and it was *warm*.

We put the bowl of food on the floor of the car, by the heater vent, and drove north on the parkway, keeping our eyes peeled for any sign of her. But you couldn't see much from the road. We decided to return once more to the hill.

"This is a fine way to spend your birthday," Daniel remarked, "chasing around in the freezing cold, searching for some old stray dog." But somehow, it seemed like an important thing to be doing, and after all, we were hardy Minnesotans, right? Once more on the hill, we could see her far off and down below, tagging along with a hiker and two dogs. And us, being dog-less as we were, I knew she wouldn't come, for that was what seemed to attract her. Anyway, by now, the food we had brought was frozen solid. We headed home and re-dressed for the mall.

It took us only ten minutes, by freeway, to reach the Mega-mall (as it had come to be known). The place was definitely grand and very glittery. There were more shops and stores than I ever care to visit in a lifetime, and excesses galore. The word "decadent" comes to mind. It was fun, and besides, parking was a snap.

Although I had never given the animal much thought before, there was definitely a wolf-motif running throughout the day, as if something had crept stealthily into my consciousness. Suddenly, I saw wolves everywhere: on coffee mugs, gazing out at me from the faces of clocks, on couch pillows, small figurines of wolves in glass cases. There were statues and carvings of wolves, large and small, in all kinds of poses: a mother wolf and her pups, a lone-wolf howling, a contented-looking pair of wolves, a sleeping wolf. There were wolves on key-chains and calendars. I exercised restraint. At the Nature Store, I bought a t-shirt that had three rows of wolves—one gray, one black, and one white—loping across the front and around the back. At one of the many bookstores, I purchased a book I had been eyeing for some time, called *Women Who Run With the Wolves*. I bought a wolf calendar. Then there was a store devoted entirely to refrigerator magnets, where I bought a tiny Coca-Cola bottle, that appeared to have the Real Thing inside; and at the Many Nations shop, I bought a *Suomi* coffee mug, in honor of my Finnish heritage. It didn't take long before I was malled-out and we left, seeing only a fraction of what there was to see.

That evening we had the traditional birthday dinner: pork chops, with a pumpkin pie to hold the candles. I never *was* a cake-eater. Hence, the saying "You can't have your cake and eat it too" had little impact on me. I'm not sure how this might have affected my future psychological development: I didn't want the blankedy-blank cake to begin with! We spent the evening debating this and other important issues. By five o'clock it was dark and the day was done. The night seemed to magnify the cold; not a creature was stirring.

VI.
The Dog-Lady

The temperature actually rose during the night. It was almost ten-above when I got up the next day. This wasn't an uncommon occurrence in the winter, as the temperature relied less on the time of day, and more on the sky-cover and prevailing air mass: a clear sky usually meant cold temperatures; a thick cloud cover helped to hold the heat in. But in the winter, a good cloud cover also usually meant precipitation of one kind or another, so pick your poison. I got up and started the coffee. It was about seven-thirty. Soon, Daniel was up and we were off to the river with a bowl of food for the stray.

"Is that a working-dog?" a voice called to us from across the picnic ground, commenting, I gathered, on the black, fleece-lined harness that Bandit wore, with the chrome rings on either side. It was a woman all bundled up in hat and scarf, parka, snow pants and Sorel boots, with just her eyes and the bridge of her nose exposed; and we were all dressed in similar attire. Though the temps weren't bad, the wind had a nasty bite to it.

"No," I replied, and then said good-naturedly, "he's just a knucklehead," referring to his sled-dog mentality, that caused him to pull so hard at the leash, for so many years, that he eventually developed a large, golf-ball sized cyst on his throat, which had to be excised, because it was forever being irritated by his collar, which made us resort to using a harness on him, and left me to wonder why we hadn't done it years earlier. But of course, I didn't tell her all of that, though she laughed anyway, at the reference.

"Have you seen a stray dog hanging around here?" she asked, looking over the edge of the hill. She was accompanied by a brown and white English springer and a tall, lean, black dobie-mix who were, along with Bandit, engaged in a salutatory sniffing party. I told her that we hadn't seen the animal yet today, but had seen her on previous occasions. The woman, whose name turned out to be Clarrise, informed us that she had first come upon the pup last Saturday. She had been back daily with food, as had (we would come to find out) many other people. She called the animal Soho. "So-o-o-oho-o-o-o," she called out across the river, her voice a lilting falsetto. "Brea-ea-eakfa-a-ast!"

I kept from saying too much, until I could judge her friend or foe. Daniel had taught me this cautiousness about people: where I assumed good intent, he was always the suspicious one; together we achieved a healthy balance. And besides (and to my surprise), I was already feeling very protective of this young wolf-cub, or dog—this canine-like thing creature. But the woman seemed harmless and genuinely concerned for the animal's welfare. We all voiced our distress at the predicament the creature found itself in. Her distrust of people was blatant, and though she badly needed help, it could not be given. How could she possibly survive in this environment and in these extreme conditions on her own?

"If someone could get a hold of her, we would be willing to take her in," I heard a voice say, then realized, it had come from me. I looked at Daniel, a little surprised. He seemed to agree. Often lately, we had discussed the subject of getting another dog. I suppose we thought it might make Bandit's passing easier to take, but that would be for us, not for him, and it just didn't seem fair to bring another dog into the picture at this point. He had been a lone entity for a long time. He wasn't very patient with strangers in his house, though we had babysat for our friend's black, female shepherd, Katie-the-dog, over Christmas, and that had gone all right (though she was extremely territorial, and had us all toeing the line by the end of the week), so I knew it was possible. But to go out and actively seek a new dog, it just didn't seem right. When the time is right to have another dog, I would assure Daniel, one will come along. And so we satisfied ourselves with that.

"How 'bout if I give you my phone number, and if somebody does get her in hand, and they're not interested in keeping her, give me a call. We'll take her in." I was very conscious of not stepping on anyone's toes. I was the newcomer, it seemed, and really had no idea of the particulars: maybe someone else had already laid claim to the elusive piper. And that was fine. But the animal needed help, and if no one else was about to provide it, we would.

"That would be great!" she said brightly, assuring me that she knew of no one who was prepared to take the animal in, and she seemed to know a lot more about it than we. She couldn't keep her: there were already too many four-legged friends running around her house, she confessed. So it was done. We agreed to leave our name and number on her dashboard—it was the gray Plymouth up in the lot. I glanced around to see if Bandit was still with us or if he had wandered off, as he was so prone to do. The wolf/dog had discreetly joined the group. She had come silently and without notice. Bandit wasn't far off. I watched her cavorting with the dobie-mix. Her movements were bewitching. She was flawless and soundless. For a moment I watched her, transfixed.

"There you are!" Clarrise scolded her, and placed the food she had brought on the frozen ground, herding her dogs away so the animal could eat. Soho, as Clarrise called her, sniffed at the food, but seemed more interested in the companionship than it, and soon was back to play. We continued on our way, leaving Clarrise to chortle at the stray, admonishing her dogs not to eat Soho's food, believing her to be in good stead.

That night as I drifted off to sleep, I thought of the name that I would call her: Koko. It had good sharp *k*-sounds, and though I don't know from what source the name came, somehow, it seemed to fit.

VII.
"Lucky"

Bandit's namesake was a small and spunky, white, snub-nosed cartoon dog that appeared on "The Adventures of Johnny Quest," an animated series that used to air on Saturday mornings. The main characters in the show were Dr. Quest, a scientist whose job would take them to the far reaches of the globe; Race Bannon, his assistant, bodyguard and Johnny's tutor; Johnny, Dr. Quest's son, a blond-headed adolescent; and Hadji, a boy about Johnny's age, of Indian descent, who wore a turban and possessed some remarkable powers of illusion. And of course, the ever-comical Bandit. (Dr. Zin was the everpresent evil antagonist.) Bandit, the cartoon dog, was a big dog born to a small dog's body, going boldly where no dog has gone before, always biting off more than he could chew. Though the two Bandits were nothing alike in appearance, they were in character and their antics were similar. And so he got the name.

We lived in a large, basement efficiency unit when Daniel first brought Bandit home. We were car-less at the time—the only "wheels" we had were a pair of ten-speeds. Daniel often met me after work for the ride home. On this fateful day in June, he stopped by to visit a former neighbor, while I rode on ahead. I had just gotten cleaned up and changed, and had just sunk down into the big, square easy-chair to put my feet up when the back door opened a crack, and then closed. I didn't see anything at first, but as my eyes traveled the length of the door to the floor, there was the cutest and furriest little speck of a dog I had ever seen. He was a golden color, like the dull leaves of Autumn. He had a small white face, straight up ears, and a little curly-Q of a tail. He was barely a handful as I scooped him up, and tickled my face with his puppy fur, smelling his puppy smell. His little pin-sharp teeth tickled on my thumb. His eyes showed no fear or hesitation, only excitement and eagerness. He wriggled and fought as I giggled and cooed. Then Daniel walked in. "How do you like him?" he asked innocently.

I quickly put the puppy down and said, in my sternest voice, "We can't have a puppy here!" But I knew he knew that. The puppies were slated to go to the pound if no one took them, Daniel explained. He was one of a litter of seven, no particular breed, but there was definitely some husky or samoyed mixed in. The owner had offered Daniel an irresistible deal: if it doesn't work out, just bring him back. Sounded fair enough. I decided he could stay, but just for the night. It was a small, six-unit building we lived in, with the caretaker on the premises, and we would be fooling ourselves if we thought we could hide a dog here. But we did, for awhile.

Since our windows sat at ground level, being in the basement as we were, Bandit's house-training consisted of being shoved out the bathroom window, tethered by a string. He adapted to it easily, and never had an accident in the house. He would dig little pint-sized holes under the clothesline though, which we would hurriedly try to fill in before they were discovered. This may be what led to our final undoing.

Bandit soon learned to ride in a plastic milk-crate, strapped to the rack, on the back of the bike. There was always one or the other of us with him, and he went everywhere with us. He was afraid of nothing and would leap headlong into any situation, with no thought to the consequences. His first bout with misfortune came at an early age, as he went diving head-first into a tall stand of grass, which also happened to house a bee's nest. He came out yelping and hollering. He wore a popsicle-stick splint on his ear for several days thereafter, to keep it from drooping over permanently. I chalked his impulsive behavior up to puppy naivete and inexperience, but as it turned out, Bandit would always be long in spirit, but dangerously short when it came to common sense. He was time and again, his own worst enemy.

One day, Daniel was riding home after accompanying me to work, when Bandit fell out of the crate. Daniel had neglected to tie him in, assuming common sense would keep him in place, plus the fact that he was so small, he could barely climb over the side. But he did, as Daniel was traveling along at a good clip, and fell to the pavement, where he lay screaming in immediate agony. Daniel sat on the curb and held him until the screaming stopped, then gingerly carried him home. Bandit was not along when Daniel met me after work that day. He worriedly told me about the accident and we rushed home. I was anguished. We had no money for a trip to the vet. He was in a lot of pain, but nothing seemed to be broken. All I could do was comfort the poor little guy, and soothe him to sleep. He woke up screaming once during the night, and I was sure our discovery was imminent. But his call was so plaintive and wailing it was hard to determine its source, and no word was ever mentioned by the other tenants. Soon, Bandit was recuperated, and having outgrown the milk-crate, took to running alongside the bike. (I think this injury is the one that has come back to haunt him now, in his old age.) We soon found a house for rent on the other side of town, near the river, with a fenced yard. It was perfect for a dog. We gave up the bikes and acquired a car.

Bandit's loyalty would always be with whatever lay around the next bend (he would have made an excellent sled-dog). You could stay behind, or try to keep up. He came when called only if it suited him, his nose and yearnings were his master and guide. He would go with anyone, anywhere, anytime, the operative word being "go." He was a hard one to keep track of. One day when I got home from work, the back gate was open and Bandit was gone. We'd had him for just over a year.

We spent days combing the neighborhood, calling for him at the river, putting up wanted posters, but it was no use. We placed an ad in the Sunday paper, offering a large reward. As the days turned into over a week, I had all but given up hope of ever finding him again, and my heart was broken. Through sheer persistence, and dogged determination, we finally located him at a home in a far southeastern suburb. It's a long, tedious story, how my detective work finally paid off, which I will not go into here. Suffice it to say, he was totally unimpressed by our reunion, and would have gone again with the first neighborhood kid who would open the gate for him, had we not put cable locks on the front and back. And his willingness to bolt through any open door or gate to travel would cost him again.

The house we were living in had gone up for sale. One day, while we were both at work, the realtor came by with some potential buyers. When Daniel got home, he found Bandit barely able to stand, his legs were swollen and wobbly. He found the business card the agent had left, lying on the dining-room table, and he was immediately suspect. He called the man's number. Apparently, Bandit had shot past the agent when he opened the door (which was hard to imagine, because the house had an enclosed front porch, and there would have been two doors to go through) and into the street, right into the side of a passing automobile. Daniel was fuming; the agent had left no notice of the event at the house, which would have been the proper thing to do. All the man had to say was, "Couldn't you keep the dog in the garage during the day?" Daniel assured him, we could not, and there would be no more house-showings in our absence. In a few days, Bandit was back to his old self. If the timing had been a little different, and the car had hit Bandit, instead of Bandit hitting the car, the result, I'm sure, would have been tragic.

When Bandit was two-and-a-half we moved Up North. I was lucky to get a high-paying union job at a paper mill in the more northern part of the state (mostly through the advantage of nepotism), and it seemed like a good move for all of us. Bandit would finally have the space he needed to run, and we could get a fresh start. I wasn't ready to give up on the city forever, but we needed a change. We found a small, rustic farmhouse for rent and settled in. The house sat on sixty acres of its own, and was surrounded by woods and swamps. It sat far back on the property, and was invisible from the road; it was secluded and private. Our main source of heat was the wood stove in the kitchen, which we would huddle around when the winter winds took to howling. One of the out-buildings housed a sauna, also fueled by wood, which we put to good use. We immersed ourselves in the culture and climate of northern Minnesota. It seemed like the ideal setting for Bandit. But our dream of a better life for him would soon turn into a nightmare.

We had lived there only a few months. It was right after the end of deer-hunting season. Bandit had been tied-up for its duration. (I knew that some hunters had no qualms about shooting a dog, if their intended victim, the elusive white-tail, was unavailable.) Even though I kept him under close scrutiny, he wore a red bandana just in case, to signal the fact that he was *not* game. (He still got away from me on occasion.) But hunting season was over, and on this fateful morning, Daniel let Bandit out, as usual. Bandit would disappear for a time, but would always return, and could usually be summoned by a call or whistle. When he'd been gone for awhile (it seemed like longer than usual), Daniel went to check on him. He opened the porch door and found Bandit, leaning against the aluminum storm-door, with blood everywhere.

"Something's wrong with Bandit!" Daniel cried, and hearing the panic in his voice, I ran to see. I scooped Bandit up and brought him into the kitchen and began combing through his thick fur to find the source of the blood. I parted the fur on his neck to expose a big, gaping hole.

"We need to get him to the vet *now*!" I told Daniel, who was hopeless in a crisis situation, especially if it involved blood. "Go get the car!" I instructed him. Bandit was failing and going into shock. I held him in my arms for the agonizing twenty minute ride to town, which took only ten. "Hang on, boy," I told him, "hang on." The doctor was reluctant to treat him, without a fifty dollar advance payment (I guess he was afraid that Bandit might die and he wouldn't be paid for his services), but he was the only vet in town, and fortunately, the jacket I had grabbed on the way out of the house had my wallet in it, with just enough cash to cover the cost. "He better not die!" Daniel threatened him. I herded Daniel out of the office and into the car. There was nothing left to do but wait. Bandit was critical, but he survived.

Bandit came home the next day, a drawn and ghostly shadow of himself. His neck had been shaved extensively (it would take two years for his coat to fully return), and he had drainage tubes hanging out on either side of a seven-inch long sutured wound. He'd been shot with a shotgun, the vet said, and had he been struck another inch, either way up or down, he would most surely be a dead dog. His recovery was long and slow, but eventually he did recover, and became once more the maniac he had always been. But his running days were over. We were forced to build him a pen. We placed his doghouse under the branches of a tall pine and put a fence around it. Now, Bandit looked at the world through two-inch square, wire mesh. It was no way for him to live. What we thought would be a good thing for him, turned out to be very bad. We made our fortune, and in a few years, returned to the city and a house by the river. It was good to be back.

Neither was I born or raised in Minneapolis, but somehow it felt like home. During my wanderings, I left and came back to it more than once. I loved the city's vitality and diversity, and especially, its anonymity. The people, in general, are hard-working and down-to-earth, polite, and respectful of each other. Saint Paul is the more provincial of the two; Minneapolis, the more progressive and free-thinking: after all, its people are descended from the ones who dared to cross the Mighty River, way back when. Bandit loved it, and he loved the river. He was a city-dog, born and raised.

When Bandit first came to stay with us as a puppy, we learned that his name had originally been "Lucky." You could look at it either way, he was either very lucky, or very unlucky, but in either case, it was his indomitable spirit and tremendous heart that brought him back from the brink, time after time, and his yearning for "just one more time around the block." And it is these qualities that would see him through yet another winter, one of the longest and coldest I can remember.

VIII.
Away in a Manger

The temperature was near zero when we went to the hill the next morning. An inch of snow had fallen during the night. The wind whipped out of the north, creating a wind chill temperature of twenty-five below. When we reached the picnic ground, there was Koko, curled up in a tight ball, lying unprotected in the middle of the clearing amidst the blowing snow. She raised her head and watched as we approached. As soon as we crossed the invisible line that marked her comfort zone, she jumped up, leaving an icy dent in the spot where she had been lying. We stopped.

"Hi, Koko," I greeted her, trying out the new name. She brightened when she saw Bandit. She stretched dramatically, then came bouncing toward him with her front legs waving back and forth, a comical grin on her face. Bandit greeted her stiffly. So thoroughly, it was then that she stole my heart.

I have loved dogs ever since I was a puppy, lapping up milk from a bowl my mother would place on the kitchen floor for me. I would approach her on all fours, barking and wagging my invisible tail, begging persistently until she would finally acquiesce, and fix me a saucer of milk: one for me, and one for our boxer, Boots, who was my senior by only a couple of months. He always finished first (having the biggest tongue), but never nosed-in on my portion, always waiting patiently until I'd had enough.

I mostly felt odd and alone during my growing up, trying hard to fit in, but never quite succeeding. I often found solace and comfort in the fur of my four-legged friend, the family dog, relying on that companionship to relieve my feelings of isolation. There was an easiness and acceptance to the relationship that I found nowhere else. I truly felt akin to the canine spirit. So it was only natural that I should take such an interest in this animal, whose blood ran warm and whose heart beat as surely as my own. She was so lost and alone. She was a stranger in a strange land. A wolf in the city, it was a hard thing to be.

We placed the bowl of food on the ground and stood a respectful distance away. She nosed it casually and took a couple of bites, but that was all. More, she wanted to play, and tried to provoke Bandit, but he was too busy checking his traps.

"I'll play!" I told her, and began hopping from foot to foot, spinning and falling, advancing and retreating. She looked quizzical at first, but once she got the jist of the game, tentatively began to join in. I would take a couple of steps toward her, and just when she was ready to flee, I would back off and run away, to hide behind a tree. As she came to investigate, I would pop out, and she would retreat. She soon understood it was all in fun (that I was *not* trying to trick her) and the game took on a little intensity. But she was easily spooked, so I was careful not to intimidate her.

Suddenly, Koko stopped. Her body poised motionless, except for the slight quivering of her nose. Her eyes stared off into a void, toward the opposite hill. I stopped and listened. Soon I heard a commanding voice shouting, "Come!" and "Heel! Heel!" I had an idea who it was. The closer they got, the louder the shouting. Koko stood very still.

When the man and his two black labs appeared on the other side of the clearing, Koko lunged forward. Apparently, she knew this troupe. I knew the man in passing. His dogs were always in training, hunting dogs they were, and responded to a blown whistle. Sometimes they wore radio collars to guide them. I had often seen him here in the Fall, working with the dogs. He would toss his decoy bag into the brush, sometimes a little too close to Bandit and me for my comfort (I suppose to test the dog's focus, although I hadn't *offered* to be a training device), while his dog waited at the ready. Then with a gesture from him, the dog would be off to retrieve the item. And you know how labs are, very single-minded. That dog would not stop searching for that bag, either until it was recovered, or the Earth opened up and swallowed him whole. (Bandit had no interest in retrieving. If you threw a ball for him and told him to Fetch!, he would give it an obligatory glance in passing, as he raced by it and disappeared from view.) But this man *demanded* obedience from his animals. And for the most part, they obliged. As Koko raced toward them, "Stay!" he commanded them, "stay!" But Koko was very provocative, and he soon released them to play. Bandit was obviously intimidated by the big, black dogs and kept his distance. We greeted each other casually.

"That dog is living here," he informed us authoritatively, which seemed to be his whole attitude, and made me bristle. (As it turned out, although loud and gruff, he was a very nice man.) "No one can catch her. She's a goner for sure in this weather," he concluded. Then he began shouting commands at his dogs again, and they were off. Koko took to following them, but the man shooed her away.

"Come on, Koko!" I beckoned her, slapping my hand on my leg.

"Cocoa?" the man turned incredulously, as if he'd just heard the stupidest thing in his entire life, then proclaimed, "Well, that's not much of a name for a wild thing like that!" I was a little embarrassed, and explained to him the spelling I'd perceived, but couldn't explain why I called her that. He shook his head and strode away.

Koko came back and we played some more tag. But the cold was numbing, and my fingers and toes were begging for relief. Daniel and Bandit were uncomplaining, but it was time to go. We continued down the far side of the hill and back through the glen. Koko tagged along. This time, she followed us right up the hill to the parking lot. She watched as we loaded Bandit into the backseat of the car, craning her neck, exploring everything with her eyes.

"Does Koko want to go for a ride?" I asked her, and held the door open so she could see in, and for a moment, I thought she might be considering it. But, no way! She watched and looked, this way and that, but was not about to venture so much as an inch closer. By then, my fingers and toes were throbbing and we had to go; Bandit was getting impatient in the backseat. As we drove away I watched Koko looking after the car. Then she turned and headed back down the hill.

The weather prediction was grim. They were forecasting lows near twenty-below that night, with wind chills ranging from minus-fifty to minus-sixty. I fretted for the wayward pup. I pictured her lying on that frozen tundra, in the ferocious wind, unprotected: I would bring her some straw. Daniel thought it was an excellent idea.

We always had a bale of straw on hand, for that was the key to Bandit's winter survival: it had seen him through many a cold season. I thought I would also bring her a tempting treat, so I cut a wiener into several chunks and put the pieces into a sandwich bag. I went out to the garage and threw several leafs of straw into a large, green trash-bag. Once my hands and feet had thawed out, I headed for the hill. This time, Bandit and Daniel stayed behind—they'd had enough of the great outdoors.

Koko wasn't there when I arrived. I could see by the depression left in the snow where she had been lying and decided to make her bed there, as she seemed most comfortable with that spot. Her logistics were good: though she was dead-set in the middle of the clearing, out in the open, it was an excellent vantage point. She could see in every direction and detect an approaching threat, before it was upon her. From that spot, she could also see clear across the valley, to the opposite hill, where the cars parked and the people came from. I wasn't worried about placing her out in the open like that, since only the die-hards would come here in this weather, and apparently, her presence was no secret to any of them.

I shook the straw out into a big, loose pile, arranging and rearranging it, until it looked inviting. Just then, a gust of wind caught the empty trash bag. I lunged after it, startling Koko, who had been standing no more than ten feet away, watching. Once again, I had neither seen nor heard her arrive. I looked around, wondering where she had come from. But standing now, in the middle of the hill, it could have been from any direction. Her presence seemed unbounded by time or space.

"So, what do you think?" I asked her, then backed away so she could inspect the pile. She stepped gingerly into the straw, sniffed in it, pawed at it, turned several circles, then lay down. She seemed to approve. I took the bag out of my pocket, with the wiener bites inside, and offered her one. She was immediately suspicious, and bolted from the straw. She stood a fair distance away and watched me intently. I approached a small step. She stood her ground. I approached another step, holding the tasty morsel out to her. I could tell by her expression that I was pressing the line. She was still more than a dozen feet away. I tossed the treat a couple of feet in front of her nose and stood very still. The cold was beginning to penetrate my umpteen-layers of clothing. I shivered. Koko jumped. I backed off a couple more feet, and coaxed her to take the treat I had thrown. Eventually she did, keeping her eyes on me the whole time.

"Good girl!" I congratulated her, and threw another treat, a little closer. Now she was hyper-suspicious. She paced back and forth, unable to make any headway toward the tempting treat. I could see her anxiety flourishing. She was in a quandary. "Oh, Koko," I commiserated with her, "it's no big deal. Here," I told her, and laid the rest of the treats on the ground for her. "It's too damn cold to be playing games, huh?" I said, and backed away until she felt safe enough to come forward and snatch the treats.

I talked to her awhile longer, but my fingers were burning again and every step I took sent a searing pain from the soles of my feet to my knees. I hated to leave her, but I had to go. Koko watched me disappear over the edge of the hill. Then she settled back into her straw, as the night and cold settled upon her.

IX.
Trial by Ice

The next morning, I plopped myself down in the chair and clicked on The Weather Channel, but I already knew it was bad. The wind had been rattling the windows all night and the furnace was cranking constantly. I was right. It was nineteen-below. There was an ill wind blowing out of the north, creating wind chills between sixty and seventy-five below. The wind chill advisories had turned into warnings, which basically just meant another layer of clothes. The formidable Siberian Express was bearing down upon the land, leaving nothing in its wake but a freeze-dried world. Nothing moved that didn't have to; cars wouldn't start and schools closed. Bandit would surely be needing his footgear today.

Bandit barked and danced and struggled. I pleaded and cajoled and scolded, and finally managed to wrestle him into his blue felt boots with the Velcro closures. He hated it; not so much the boots, as the fact that he was being restrained.

"Bandit," I tried to explain patiently, "if you don't put your boots on, we can't go for a walk," but of course, the only word he understood there was "walk," which only made him all the more excited and full of angst. And I still had to get me dressed. I already had sweatpants and long underwear on, underneath my jeans, and a heavy pair of socks on. I added a pair of thermal socks to those and a sweatshirt and sweater over my turtleneck and t-shirt. I wrapped a heavy scarf around my neck and up over my face, put on my down vest, and then my hooded parka. I pulled my Sorels on and laced them up. I put my Yazoo cap on, ear-flaps down, and grabbed my thick, insulated, leather snowmobile gloves. Bandit yammered away at me the whole time. Daniel went to start the car while I put some wiener bites into a sandwich bag, for the stray. I was anxious to see how she had survived the frigid night.

As we crested the hill, Koko raised her head from her bed of straw. Her eyelashes and muzzle were heavy with frost. This morning, she looked cold.

"Hey, Koko," I greeted her. "How's the wild-wolfer doin' today?" She got up and stretched, arching her back, pointing her muzzle toward the sky. We waited as she got herself together and blinked the sleep from her eyes. She stepped lightly from the straw and advanced toward Bandit. He was zig-zagging along, nose to the frozen ground, with his leash dragging along behind.

When I did let Bandit go, I often left his leash hooked onto his harness, for an added measure of safety. He was easier to grab a hold of, should a situation develop, and with Bandit, that could be at any time. When he got it into his head to go, he *went*, and no amount of shouting would bring him back. Daniel often applauded my ability to anticipate his actions, and my agility to dive for the leash and grab hold, at the last possible moment. I wasn't much of a disciplinarian, I do confess, and when I did try to be strict with Bandit, he would just give me that patronizing look, and try to gauge the seriousness of my request, then either continue on with whatever he was doing or meander off in the other direction. When he did obey, I think it was just to humor me. (But however undisciplined he was, his manners were impeccable.) Often times, I found myself relishing in his disobedience. After all, he was a dog, and dogs will be dogs, no matter what, the animal whose quintessential nature and guileless spirit I so admired.

Koko slunk toward Bandit with her head lowered, touching his muzzle from underneath with hers, emitting the slightest whimper and whine. Then she slammed her rump against his shoulder and encircled him, her own nose almost touching her tail on his other side, in effect, wrapping herself around him. They were nearly equal in size, though where he was stout, she was long. She could bend and crane her body into the most extraordinary poses; her movements were disjointed and flowing. Bandit stood patiently for the greeting, but once released, proceeded on to inspect, and lift his leg on, her bed of straw. Koko followed behind him, keenly interested in the apparel he wore on his feet. She started out sniffing, but soon began tugging on his boot, attempting to extricate it, much to Bandit's chagrin. Having no luck with that, she grabbed the leash in her mouth, and began pulling Bandit in circles around the hill. He followed obediently, but barked in protest. Daniel and I cracked up. Bandit looked at me, pleading for help.

I didn't want to come off scolding, so I did the next best thing. I took the bag of treats from my pocket, and rattled it noisily. It worked. Koko's attention was drawn and she dropped the leash. She approached cautiously, staying several feet away, as I offered her a treat. She watched warily as I tossed the treat directly under her nose. She jumped back a bit, then stepped forward and greedily snatched up the treat. I tossed another, a couple of feet closer. She went for it easily. Now I also had Bandit's attention. I planted my feet firmly and reached out as far as I could, with the treat in my hand, coaxing her to take it. She leaned forward, and with her neck and hind legs stretched out as far as they could go, nosed the wiener bite in my hand, but wouldn't take it. At that point, Bandit had had enough. He butted in and snatched the treat directly from my hand. I pulled out another one. Koko was getting anxious and moved in closer, goaded by the competition. I held it out to her. By now, my fingers were on fire, burning from the cold and the wind and the wiener juice. But I maintained. Just as Bandit was about to make his move, like lightning, Koko reached in and grabbed the treat from my hand, delivering a solid nip to my frozen fingers in the process. She was back standing away, in the blink of an eye. My pain was pacified only by my excitement.

"Did you see that?" I asked Daniel, stuffing my throbbing fingers into my coat pocket. Of course he had, and urged me to try again. I offered Bandit a treat, which he readily took, then offered another to Koko. She knew the game now. As Bandit moved in, she lurched forward and snatched the treat right out from under his nose, nipping my fingers again in the process. "Yoweee!" I cried out, involuntarily, which made Koko retreat several more steps and stare at me curiously. Bandit liked this game, treats *and* a walk, but I had had enough. My fingers couldn't stand another assault. I dumped the remaining treats on the ground and gave Bandit his cut.

It seemed we had made some progress, though I wasn't sure to what end. It was true, I had succeeded in getting her to take food from my hand, but I could no more grab a hold of her than I could the wind, so what had really been accomplished? She knew what my intentions were, and had no intention of giving herself up for a mere morsel of food. Her actions, it seemed, were guided less by fear, and more by a severe mistrust that seemed almost inherent in her nature.

I could tell that Bandit was getting tired. Daniel was stalwart but my fingers and toes were screaming in agony. The sixty-below wind chill had me in retreat. We decided to head for home, catch a brief warm-up, then return with a bowl of food, which we had neglected to bring. (I was still surprised to see her every morning, though it had been five days since.) Soon, Clancy arrived with his owner and we made our exit. By nine that morning we were back.

The sun was just starting to inch up over the trees across the river. The sky was pink and red on the horizon and a brilliant blue overhead. There was not a cloud in view; the day would not warm much. Koko was back in her straw when we arrived. She jumped up as we approached. I placed the warm bowl of food next to her bed, so she could stand in the straw while she ate. We backed off. Just as she was about to indulge, suddenly, her head shot up. Her body was fixed and poised, her ears at attention; her eyes stared intently toward the opposite hill. She posed an elegant statue. I followed her gaze and could discern through the bare trees, the familiar gray Plymouth, way across in the parking lot. Soon the melodic "So-o-o-oho-o-o-o," drifted up on a breeze. Clarrise came trudging up the hill.

"Oooh," she said, "I like the straw idea!"

"Yeah, she seems to like it," I said.

Clarrise cooed and prattled on to Koko, "How ya doin' today, girlie? Didja have a rough night? Poor baby . . . " until Koko returned to her interrupted meal. We commiserated about the weather and watched Koko eat. Clarisse had brought some dry-crunch in a plastic bag, which she laid open near the straw bed. She had left her dogs home today. It was just too cold.

"I didn't get my coffee this morning," Clarrise said in an exaggerated, whining voice, then explained that their pipes had frozen up during the night. I looked at Daniel, trying to sense his persuasion. We guarded our privacy zealously and, by Daniel's superstitious nature, were not prone to inviting strange people into our home. But, no coffee! This was an emergency!

"When we leave here, why don't you come by for a cup?" I offered, and looked at Daniel, who seemed to agree. She thought for a moment, then said, "Great! That would be great!" I told her we had a magnetic heater that she might be able to use on her frozen pipes, if I could only locate it. "That's great!" she said enthusiastically. "That's really nice of you," she said. We smiled.

"She has a place down there where she stays," Clarrise said, pointing over the side of the cliff. "We brought a temporary shelter down for her to use," she continued, "I'll take you and show you where if you like. I'm anxious to see if she's used it."

Her helpfulness was a little bit unnerving: her willingness to give away the location of Koko's secret place to us, who she hardly knew. (I hoped it was only because we seemed so trustworthy.) But we followed along, with Koko happily in tow. I felt a little guilty and reluctant to invade the animal's privacy, but I was intrigued.

"The best way down is over there," Clarrise said, and pointed toward the other end of the hill, "there's a path."

I knew it well. In Bandit's younger days, we had often ventured down-below. There were several paths between here and Lake Street that would take you to the bottom, all of which were steep, some more treacherous than others. We walked to the other end of the picnic ground, and down the hill to the valley. We hopped the fence that guarded the edge of the hill there, to land on the path that would take us down. As it turned out, the best way to navigate the icy slope, was to slide down the trail on your tail, using your feet out in front, to break your speed, grabbing at rocks, limbs or roots on the way down, for added assurance. There was a sheer, ten-foot drop at the bottom. We laughed at ourselves as we slid down the steep embankment.

"Wheee-ee-ee!" Clarrise shrieked. Koko bounded along effortlessly; she seemed nonplussed.

There was an immense silence down-below. Who could even guess at the teeming city above? We were the intruders into this quiet place, our boots crunching in the snow, imposing on the calm. Our breath formed a frosty chorus of clouds in the frozen air. The large chunks of ice, piled haphazard on the shore, told a version of the river's power. A big, black crow, perched high in a tree, warned of our arrival. Caw! Caw! it spoke; and Koko took notice. She stared at the crow with intent, as if to decipher its call. The ice on the river heaved and moaned, betraying the flood of water that flowed underneath.

We walked the flatland below, back toward the place we had been up above, with the river to our right, the shale and limestone cliffs to the left, climbing over fallen trees and picking our way through the rocks. Clarrise stopped and pointed to a ledge, high up in the cliffs. "It's up there," she said. She was standing beside the Styrofoam doghouse they had brought: it was a four-sided box, lined with blankets, with a small opening on one side. She'll never go in there, I thought.

"She's been here! She took the bait we left!" Clarrise said excitedly, looking into the dark doorway. "We put some blankets up there for her too," she said, pointing up the cliff. "I'd like to go see if it looks like she's been there, but I don't know if these knees of mine will let me." Daniel and I offered to make the climb.

I set my Yazoo cap on the doghouse. It had a tendency to fall off when the ear-flaps were unfastened, and it was hard to hear with them down. We climbed up the steep and slippery side of the cliff, using roots and branches for hand and footholds. I grabbed at the rocks and pulled myself up and onto the ledge that Koko called home. Now I really felt like an intruder. I saw two rumpled blankets that definitely looked used.

"Looks like she's been here!" I called down to Clarrise, wondering how her and husband Norman had ever found this place. I glanced down just in time to see Koko making off with my cap. "Hey!" I shouted and pointed. Clarisse went shrieking after Koko, who immediately dropped her prize. Clarrise retrieved it while Koko stood a safe distance away, looking on.

I sat on the ledge and looked around. The view was impressive: the frozen Mississippi below stretched out to the north and faded to the south. I could see Koko's footprints in the snow, leaving the ledge on either side. Her tracks appeared all in a straight line. I attempted to follow her trail as it rose, then followed precariously along the edge of the cliff beside the fence, to a place where it was low enough that she could easily hop over, and make her way to the picnic area above.

Then I understood how she could mysteriously appear out of nowhere. She could probably hear from the ledge, the sounds from above, alerting her to the fact that company had arrived. She could easily make her way along the edge of the cliff, unobserved, to come up anywhere at the picnic ground, even standing undetected in the trees, waiting for just the right moment, to make her silent entrance.

Not wanting to invade her space any longer, we made our descent, grabbing at roots and limbs, gaining momentum on the way, until we landed in a solid heap at the bottom. "Very graceful," Clarrise commented. We all laughed. The trek back up to the top of the gorge proved to be much more of a challenge than the trip down, sudden fits of laughter threatening to foil any progress we made. We finally reached the top, huffing and puffing, collapsing on the ice-covered ground, exhausted. Koko thought it was all great fun. I would have laughed more, but my feet were so frozen, I wanted to cry.

After a quick rest, we picked ourselves up and continued our trek to the parking lot. Koko followed us up to the waiting cars. Again, we tried to coax her in, but to no avail. I told Clarrise our address, and reluctantly we left, with Koko standing and staring mournfully on. My heart ached for her. It seemed like she wanted to come, but somehow, just couldn't.

X.
A Legend in Her Own Time

We pulled into the alleyway and into the garage just as Clarrise arrived out front. Bandit was curled up in his straw, under the kitchen window, just shy of the cold sun. He raised his head and wagged his tail noncommittally as we crossed the yard, but didn't get up. I tried to coax him to come inside with us, but he wouldn't budge.

"You'll be coming in soon!" I threatened him. He looked at me as if to say, we'll see about that! Though he looked comfortable enough, I worried about him staying out in these temps for too long. He was smart enough to come in out of the rain (thunder was the only thing in the world that truly rattled him; you could always tell when a summer storm was approaching by the way he behaved: "The Bandometer says rain," we would say, as he shirked through the house, cowering and trying to stay close), but he relished in the cold and snow. Sometimes, I would find him curled up in his straw, trying not to, but shivering just the same. Then I would grab him by the collar and tell him, "That's it bud, you're in," and drag him inside, kicking and growling, and barking in protest all the way. He would lie on his rug in the dining-room, glaring at me, for all of ten minutes. Then he would be up and at the back door again, whining and yapping to go out. I would put him off for as long as possible, but he was persistent and I was weak, and eventually I would give-in, and out he would go again, to resume his vigil, curled up in the straw in his triangle, waiting for the next walk to commence.

I went through the house to let Clarrise in the front door. Daniel was in the kitchen, starting a fresh pot to brew.

"I gotta get these boots off," Clarrise moaned, "my feet are dying."

I cranked up the furnace and we began to shed some of our garb. Off came the parkas and boots, scarves and hats. Our faces were bright red from the cold. It was the first time we were really able to see each other, after being all bundled up in our winter attire. Clarrise was a robust woman, somewhere past forty, I thought. She had a willing smile and a glint in her eye, that sometimes hinted at mischief. Her manner was boisterous and familiar.

We sat with our hands and feet glued to the register, questing for immediate relief. When the coffee finished brewing, we moved back into the sun-soaked kitchen and sat at the table, with our hands wrapped around steaming mugs. We were linked by a common purpose. We talked about Koko.

"The first time I saw her," Clarrise began, "was last Saturday. A week it will be, tomorrow" (just a few days before *my* initial encounter with her). "But I know a woman who saw her as far back as Christmas Eve," she said. I counted back. That was almost three weeks ago! I thought.

The woman's name was Meryl. She had been at the hill that evening, Christmas Eve, walking her two dogs. It was a bright night, the moon nearly full, illuminating the snow. The trees cast gaunt and ghostly shadows. Out of nowhere, the animal had appeared, joining her dogs in a silent dance. She watched the phantom-like creature, cavorting in the moonlight, unsure of the apparition before her. She was struck by a feeling of benevolence, it being Christmas Eve and all. She was profoundly moved by the experience, Clarrise said, and spoke almost reverently of it. Then as quickly as she had appeared, the animal was gone. She had been back feeding her regularly ever since. She was one of Koko's night-visitors. And there was more.

Another woman, named Gail, had also been feeding her. She had also discovered her one night, while walking her dogs. Her theory was that this was a coyote, who had wandered too far up the river, and when spring came, she would surely run back down the river to mate. I would never meet either of these two people, though Clarisse would keep me apprised of their feelings. Gail had expressed her disagreement with the idea that the animal should be caught. Her feelings were that this was a wild creature, who could obviously fend for herself, and should be left to her own devices. Meryl sympathized with the animal's plight, but didn't have the resources, or it seemed the inclination, to be of any real help.

Another's theory was that this was a wolf cub, who had wandered too far *down* the river. This seemed very unlikely, as she would have had to travel right through the downtown area, following the river; and it was a long way from here to the North Country, where the wolves reside. Clarrise seemed to know all the scuttlebutt.

Someone said they knew someone who saw her get thrown from a car, that early Christmas Eve. Another reported that the animal had jumped *into* a woman's car. The lady began shrieking at her and the animal jumped out and ran off, terrified. This seemed even more unlikely, knowing Koko's aversion to automobiles.

One report claimed to have seen *two* animals, that appeared to be litter-mates. One was so shy it hid forever in the trees, while the other would romp with the neighborhood dogs that strolled by, though kept clear of their people. This had supposedly occurred somewhere *north* of the Lake Street bridge and some time around Thanksgiving. It was hard to believe she could have been on her own for so long.

In time, we would all come up with our own theories about her and her origin, and why she had chosen this particular spot to stay. Perhaps she *had* lost a litter-mate and was there waiting and hoping for his return. Or, maybe she had been dropped off at this very site, and so remained, having nowhere else to go. Daniel's theory was that she was an alien being, whose parents had died when their spaceship crashed, and so took the form of the most heroic and noble creature on the planet, *Canis lupus*. The more I got to know Koko, the more I tended to believe this scenario.

But however it came to be, the animal needed help. That was obvious, as each day I witnessed her failing: the weariness in her gait, the desperate look in her eyes as we left her each time, to face another long, frigid night alone. She had a very runny stool, and it was clear, that whatever nutrition she was taking in, she was burning it up that fast. Her health was in decline, and Clarrise thought, she probably had worms. Add to that, the vicious cold plundering the land, and it was no wonder, how all of these elements combined were slowly sapping her strength. The temperature tonight was predicted to drop to twenty-five below, and the wind chill would make it even more unbearable. How could she possibly survive? I don't know at what temperature hell freezes over, but it would take until then to get close to her there, "in the wild," at the hill. We decided, somehow we would have to catch her, either by force or trickery, and for her own sake, take her. It was only for the sake of her own survival. But how to do that? She was wise and wily beyond all time.

Clarrise suggested a noose-type device, like the thing that Animal Control used, which was basically a noose on the end of a stick, that would allow the animal to be held several feet at bay, should it become vicious once caught. It was an idea, though getting that close to her with such a contraption seemed unlikely.

Clarrise then launched into a litany of other animals that her and Norman had rescued over the years. It seemed, every year, they had their "project" animal that was rescued and restored to a happy existence. One time it was a ferret, who they found almost hairless and half-frozen in the snow. Then a neighborhood cat, who had been abandoned when its owner went into a nursing-home, came to their house to stay. And there were always dogs that strayed in and out, or ones that were loose, that she would pick up off the street and take home, to seek out the rightful owners of, or if that proved to be impossible, find new and appropriate homes for. She was definitely a Friend to the Animals, and though she seemed to me, a little overzealous in her concern, it was hard to fault her. Koko was her new interest, but she had her stumped.

We tried to think of other ways, by which we might apprehend her. Clarrise thought she might try to locate a large live-animal trap, bait it, and get her that way. Or maybe a net, she thought, camouflaged in the snow, with the ropes from it cast over the limbs of a nearby tree, to pull on at just the right second. None of these sounded too attractive. I was thinking mostly of the trauma it would cause to the animal, and the chance that if we failed, we might scare her off permanently. Koko was much too wary and alert to carelessly fall into either of these traps, I thought, but I really had nothing of my own to offer.

I went to the basement to find the magnetic heater for Clarrise's frozen pipes. We reassured her as she left, that should the animal be caught, we would definitely provide her with a home. It was no longer a question of *could* we take her in, we were *bound* to take her. It seemed to be no less than a matter of Life and Death. We were committed to supply the safety and warmth she so desperately needed. I dared to think no further than that.

XI.
To Catch a Wily Wolf

I use the term "wolf" descriptively and only for the sake of expediency. It is true, she looked and acted every bit the part, and her very being spoke of forces both primordial and wild, but her true lineage will probably never be known. And if indeed, a wolf she be (and a wild one at that), how to explain her presence here, in this urban setting? It was all just too unbelievable. I was at a loss myself, to completely accept or reject either pronouncement, although in my heart, sometimes the truth shouted plain. (Eventually would be born the saying, "If enough people call you a wolf, you'd better start howling.") One thing she was for certain, was an animal in serious trouble.

And so we whiled away the winter hours, imagining countless scenarios that could have brought her to this place. Was her distrust of people so because she had been abused? Had she been abandoned, or had she simply run away from somewhere and someone? Perhaps she had been mistreated by someone who came home once-too-often to find that she had chewed on their expensive sneakers or stereo-speakers, or made a mess on the floor (as puppies are prone to do these things when left too long to their own devices), and her punishment, after so many beatings, to be discarded by the road-side, one dark and scary night. That would explain her intense fearfulness, for violence does damage to the soul, and though the wounds might heal, scars remain—anyone who has been touched by violence knows. Or had she never been socialized with people at all, and only thought humans to be strange and random creatures? The mystery could never be solved, unless of course, Koko suddenly gained voice and chose to relate it. But obviously, that was not bound to happen.

We turned again to the problem at hand: exactly what was the best way to capture this wily creature? We dismissed most of the ideas previously discussed as too risky, considering their actual chance for success. The only one I thought even remotely feasible, was to use the noose-type device. But if it worked, it would be an all or nothing proposition. Once the animal was snared, we decided, there was *no* letting go, whatever the consequences. It would be a total disaster to let her get loose, with a noose around her neck and a length of rope trailing behind, for there would be no catching up to her again. And she would most certainly, eventually, get caught up on something and strangle herself to death. It was a grim picture.

There would be no letting go! That was the imperative—and the scary part. What if she lashed out, with gnashing teeth and slashing claws, what would I do then? What if she fought and struggled so hard, the noose tightened around her neck, and choked the very breath of life from her body? I envisioned the worst. What would I do? Well, I would gladly leap into the middle of slashing teeth and claws, and remove the noose from around her neck, whatever the cost to me. I would face the danger, rather than put it to her. But all of this was my thinking *way* too far ahead: we hadn't even come up with a plan to construct the device yet. But we had some ideas.

There was a piece of plastic pipe in the basement, though a little large in diameter, just the right length. We found a perfect piece of rope to thread through it, thick and heavy, about ten feet long. We put the rope through the plastic pipe and tied a slip-knot in one end and a large, square-knot in the other, to keep it from sliding back through the pipe. I held it out at arm's-length and dangled the noose out in front of me. I practiced tightening the noose around a gallon can of paint, held stationary. The results were promising, though looking at the device, I doubted whether Koko would have anything to do with it. I went out to try it on Bandit.

Daniel's work called and the party was over. He would be heading out that evening for Huntsville, Alabama, hopefully to be back by Monday. It was Friday. Daniel went to bed, hoping to get a few hours sleep before it was time to go. Since it was almost time for Bandit's afternoon walk, I decided to take him, and avoid the ruckus later. And besides, I wanted to see what Koko thought of her new "toy"; so I brought it along.

The high temperature that day was nine-below. The sky remained clear, and the bitter wind still blew relentlessly out of the north, as twilight reigned in. We geared up, boots for Bandit, and headed for the hill. I held the plastic noose-device, close under my arm as we walked toward the picnic ground, feeling somewhat like the thief: I was afraid someone would see the contraption and get the wrong idea, thinking I meant to do the animal harm, and who did I think I was anyway . . . ? But Koko already had visitors.

The dog had the biggest ears I'd ever seen. He was a huge, fawn-colored shepherd, with the most benign look in his eyes. Bandit had no trouble approaching him. Koko jumped and danced about, delighted with the company. The dog's name was Zack. The person with him was a woman dressed in full-length, tan, insulated coveralls. With her hat pulled down and the scarf covering her face, her features were indiscernible, though she seemed to be close to my age. Her eyes held a certain sparkle. She was throwing a stick for Zack, which Koko would run to retrieve before Zack could lumber over to it. Then she would parade in front of his nose, holding the stick high, like a baton, and swoop down with it, tempting him to try and take it. Finally, Zack would latch onto the stick, and the game would be over, making up for in mass, what he lacked in speed. He was an old guy, too, I would come to find out.

We introduced ourselves. Her name was Maryanne. Her manner was calm and reserved, otherworldly. She spoke slowly and very deliberately, as if each word had to be pulled from some unknown depth. Her face was unextraordinary, except for the twinkle in her eye and a subtle smile that cursed the corner of her mouth, as if she was privy to some inside joke, of a universal nature. Her manner caught me off guard.

"Are you going to try and catch her with that?" she asked, sincerely interested in the device I was transporting. I felt a little sheepish.

"Maybe, eventually," I stammered, "but for now, I'm just going to see what she thinks of it." It was my time at bat.

The woman obviously knew the animal's predicament, and showed no objection as I tempted Koko with the dangling rope. I had no illusions about catching her today, I just wanted to see if she would even accept the item, and then, to have her perceive it as a source of play. She was very suspicious of it, and soon I abandoned the length of plastic pipe altogether. I tossed the rope, by itself, toward her, and fished it back and forth, walking away from her, tempting her to bite. She followed behind and nosed the rope a couple of times. She pawed at it and pounced on it, and soon, took it in her mouth. I immediately let go of my end. She pranced away with her prize, holding it high, tossing it into the air and catching it. I let her bask briefly, then went in pursuit. She was easily intimidated and quickly dropped the rope, slinking away then, with her tail between her legs.

"It's okay, girl," I assured her, as I recovered the rope, then began the snake-dance again, encouraging her to take it. She was hard-pressed to resist, and was soon back on my tail, in pursuit of the swirling rope. She took it more easily this time, and when I felt her tug, I stayed on the line. As soon as Koko felt the resistance, she dropped the rope and jumped away; she stood watching thoughtfully, as the rope again moved steadily away. "Come on, Koko," I goaded her, "don't be such a woose. Get the rope! Get the rope!"

Soon we were engaged in a cautious game of tug-of-war. Too much resistance on my part would send her scurrying away. As her apprehensive tugs grew evermore assertive, I would release the rope and let her have it, as a reward. She would dash away with it in her mouth, victoriously.

By that time, another woman had joined Maryanne (who had stayed to watch the game). It was a small woman in a bright blue parka, with a molded cold-weather mask covering her face. She was an older woman, with no dog in sight. They, of course, were talking about Koko. I joined them.

"She followed me home yesterday," the woman was saying. She had been out walking with her sister and her sister's dog. She lived in one of the expensive houses along Edmund Boulevard, the winding street that paralleled West River Road, with the houses that looked toward the river. "I felt so sorry for her," she continued. "She followed me home, but wouldn't come near the house. So I brought some food outside for her." She said when she emerged again, the animal was gone. I thought this was an interesting development. She said she was worried about her, and had come back to check on her, with a can of Mighty Dog to offer. She had been watching us playing with the rope, and was happy to know that someone was trying to do something to help her out of her predicament. "I don't know how long she can last in this weather," she said, her voice grave, "and she's so terribly afraid of people."

We commiserated together on the animal's plight, and I again let it be known, that we were prepared to take her in, if someone could just get a hold of her. Everyone seemed heartened by that. We exchanged information, and I was promised that I would be contacted, if anything developed. It was amazing, just how many people were willing to give up their private information, and time, to help save this lost animal. People you would never suspect.

By now, Bandit was getting bored and was starting to drift away. It was time to move on. My feet were cold and ready to fall off. I bade farewell to Koko, promising to come back in the morning, when we could play the rope-game again. Bandit and I departed toward the far side of the hill. I stopped to fluff up her straw on the way, deciding that I should bring her some more, when I came in the morning. It was damn cold.

That night, I drove Daniel to the tractor-lot (where his truck was parked while he was in town) by way of the River Road. It was near midnight. As we passed Thirty-sixth Street, we both looked through the darkness toward the place on the hill where we knew she would be, huddled in the straw. Of course we couldn't see her there, so far away and in the dark, but I could sense her there: a speck of life, though fleeting and fragile it seemed. It would be the coldest night yet, as the temperature ranged to thirty-degrees below zero. It was inhuman, ungodly, and downright unfair.

XII.
Winter Wonderland

    I thought it best to leave Bandit home the next morning, when I went to the hill. The conditions were just too brutal. But he would still have to go somewhere, because he wouldn't "go" in the yard: his record hold-out time stands at fifty-six hours, when the conditions were just so terrible, I couldn't possibly take him out. Stubbornly he would wait and wait, and pester and wait, and pester and wait. He didn't understand why we couldn't go. I hated to put him through it, and after all, today it was only cold: we could at least make it around the block! But as soon as he took care of his business, I warned him, we were headed home. But he was savvy to that and would hold out for as long as possible, to get as many miles under his belt as he could. "Just around the block, Bandit," I would vow, and then before I knew it, we would be halfway to the river. But today, no shenanigans: it was dangerously cold.
    It took longer to get us ready, than to actually go out and do it. With the mercury steady at twenty-five below, and the winds kicking the wind chill index down into the sixty-below range, it took a lot of preparation: a lot of layers and extra care, to make sure that everything was pulled up and tucked in. If Bandit lost a boot on the way, and I had to remove my gloves to re-fit it, it was all over; it made my fingers swell just to think about it. We took it all in stride though, acclimated to it by now. But I think Bandit might have sensed the seriousness of the conditions, for he was perfunctory on his mission and soon we

were back home. I pulled his boots off, and gave him a tight hug and a kiss on the top of his head as I reached under to undo his harness (he was ever the independent fellow and didn't stand for much coddling, so I snuck it in on him when I could).

"I'm gonna have to go and check on Koko now," I told him. (I spoke to him constantly, fully aware that he could only understand about half of what I was saying.) He followed me out to the garage as I went to warm up the car, looking hopeful. "I'll be right back!" I told him, as he followed me back to the house. That was one of our "key phrases": it was my way of letting him know, that I was going and he was not; at least, that's what he understood it to mean. He retreated to his bed of straw then, to wait for the sun that would never come.

I warmed a bowl of food in the microwave, deliberately making it way too hot, hoping to get it to her before it froze. I threw several more chunks of straw into a bag and headed out. I left the rope-toy at home: this was no time to be playing games, I thought, the mode here was Survival. "I'll be right back," I told Bandit, and leaned down to pat him on his head. He watched me leave from his corner bed of straw. I should have put him in the house, I scolded myself, but I was determined to make it back quick. The temps were horrific, and after all, I was only human.

It was always quiet when we headed out, early on a weekend morning. There were no noisy school buses or kids, no rush-hour traffic, hardly any life at all, as the world slept in on a Saturday morning; and this morning, that was especially so. The world was frozen still, except for the plumes of exhaust that curled from every chimney, colored translucent pink by the rising sun. It was almost eight-thirty. I pulled into a parking space and wrapped the thick scarf up and around my face, leaving only my eyes peeking out. Cradling the warm dinner bowl next to my body and clutching the bag of straw, I headed up to see Koko. As I labored along, the condensation of my breath froze into ice crystals on my eyelashes and lower lids, so that every time I blinked, my eyes stuck shut for just a fraction of a second too long. It felt weird, but I was digging it. If you tossed a cup of boiling water up into the air, at temps not much colder than these, it would explode into a cascade of fireworks. (Although I had never actually seen it done, it was a sport practiced mostly in Northern Minnesota, where it really gets cold, I had no trouble believing it.)

I was surprised to see, as I crested the rise, that Koko was not in her bed of straw. But I was unconcerned; she could be off just about anywhere. I went about the business of refortifying her straw, expecting her to appear at any moment, as she so often did. I hoped she would come soon: the food I had brought for her was cooling off fast. I kicked around a little while longer, and when she still had not shown, scanned the bottomland for any sign of movement. There was none. I removed my glove, and with my thumb and forefinger in my mouth, let fly a shrill whistle, something to which she had responded before. It cracked the still air and echoed hard from the cliffs across the river. She could certainly hear that! I thought, and waited some more, but she never came. I strained my ears to listen: a dog barked somewhere far away; the burnt autumn leaves, that still clung stubbornly to the trees, rattled like old bones in the winter wind. No birds sang. It was rather strange, her not being there, and it felt awfully strange, her vacant bed of straw, but I still wasn't overly concerned. She had been absent before, and given enough time, would eventually show. But I just couldn't wait any longer. My feet were feeling frozen and clumsy and the little bit of my face that was exposed, was burnt and raw. I decided to relinquish and return again later, when the sun had claimed more of the sky.

I had some errands to run that morning. Bandit wasn't too happy, to be dragged inside, even though he was all shivery by the time I returned. "I'll be right back!" I told him, and pointed for him to lie down on his rug in the dining room, which he did, though he was quick to voice his discontent at being left behind again. I headed off to the mailbox and grocery store, taking advantage of the early start and already warm car. I inevitably came back by way of the River Road, and although I wasn't properly dressed, made a quick run up the hill, to see if Koko had appeared. Her straw was still empty. I had just made it through the back door, with the last load of groceries, when the phone rang. Thinking it was Daniel, I rushed to answer.

"Good mo-o-o-or-ning," a familiar voice chimed. It was Clarrise. "Say," she said, "did you by any chance go to the hill today? Did you see her? Was she there?" I told her I had been there but hadn't seen her. "I'm really worried," she said, her voice trembling a little just to prove it. "It was so *awfully* cold last night." Always the optimist, I assured her that the animal was probably holed up somewhere, though

I was beginning to wonder myself. We decided to go in shifts, to check for her arrival.

"If I don't see her," I told Clarrise, "I'll climb up to her ledge and have a look; the poor thing might have just froze to death during the night." At the thought of that, Clarrise wailed. Maybe the animal *had* just gone off to sleep, to awaken nevermore; the extreme and relentless cold had to be taking some kind of toll on her, and everyday she appeared weaker. And where was the line drawn between cold and *too* cold? Thirty-below? Sixty-below? How much could she endure? Maybe a healthy animal could survive this, but Koko was not a healthy animal. And she was alone.

I returned to the hill for the third time that day. It was high noon. The temperature stayed stubbornly at seventeen-below. The wind had died a little. Still, there was no sign of the stray. It was all too quiet and it seemed very empty without her. She had become a mainstay at this place, and her absence was keenly felt. Well, I thought, she's probably either dead or she's moved on, and though I leaned toward the latter, whatever had happened, she was gone. I allowed myself to feel briefly, the sadness and loss, but many a stray dog had crossed my path through the years, and I learned at a young and tender age, the cruel lesson, that you can't save them all. My parents were very lenient in that regard, and although we did take a couple of the strays in, that had "followed me home" (always to my mother's dismay), most were sent off with a kind word and full belly, to pursue their fortunes elsewhere. But this loss was especially difficult. I had tried so hard to win her over. If she only knew, I thought. I tried to console myself with the old adage, that things usually happen for the best.

For the lack of anything better to do, and since to keep moving was to keep warm, I decided to make the laborious journey down below and climb the cliff, up to her ledge, although I really didn't expect to find her there. And I didn't. I called and whistled a couple of times, as I walked the flatland below, but I knew if she was anywhere around, she was already well aware of my presence. She would show herself only if she chose to, and there was no dog along, to lure her out.

It was an eerie calm that lay below. I had never been down to the bottom without Bandit, and certainly, never by myself. (Since having him, it was on a rare occasion that I walked anywhere alone, and when I did, the action seemed tedious and without purpose—I felt like four of my legs were missing.) Nary a sound interrupted the silence, only the crunching of my boots in the crusted snow and the beating of one solitary heart, both amplified by the surrounding stillness. My labored breaths echoed in my skull and hung aloft, leaving a trail of steamy clouds, soon to be swallowed up by the freezing air. I thought I would keep heading north, maybe as far as the Lake Street bridge. I really didn't expect to spot her, but I wasn't yet ready to leave: there was a spooky attraction I felt to this frozen place, with the extreme cold adding an element of danger. I walked along the frozen sand dunes, that marked the river's edge (a place we would one day dub, "Koko Beach"). I headed back through the scrub and into the trees.

Then, I imagined that I was the last living person in the world, set adrift in this tundra-land. The river belched up pockets of steam beside me. The cliffs rose high to my left. The atmosphere was surreal. Then suddenly, I heard a loud *crack!*. It sounded like a branch breaking. I turned to look, but of course, no one was there. It continued to startle me, even after I realized, it was only the ice on the river, popping from the stress. I looked hard through the trees and scanned the cliffs, but could discern no movable form. Looking back at it now, it wouldn't surprise me if Koko had been there watching me the whole time. I felt alone, but strangely, not alone. Her color so camouflaged her, that if she stood perfectly still, she could easily blend into the winter landscape. I didn't quite make it to the bridge, but felt I had gone far enough: this winter wonderland was definitely losing its appeal. I headed back toward the south and the empty picnic ground.

I phoned Clarrise upon returning home, and told her about my fruitless expedition. She said she would go and check for her the next hour. She thought it would be nice if someone was there, with food and encouragement, should she return. I agreed. Clarrise was beside herself with worry and I had all but resigned myself to the fact that we had probably seen the last of her.

As I busied myself with various household chores, the phone rang again. This time it was Daniel. He was calling from someplace in Kentucky. He bragged about the balmy weather there (as he liked to do, when he was someplace warm) and asked about the stray.

"She's gone," I told him, and filled him in on all that had transpired. I could tell he was a little upset by the news.

"Oh, no," he moaned, and then tried to encourage me. "Well, she might still show, you never know," though his words had a hollow ring. He knew I was growing attached, and I could tell that he was too. "You be careful, climbing around on those cliffs down there all by yourself!" he warned. I assured him, my rock-climbing days were over for now and he needn't worry. We said good-bye, him promising to call again later that night. It was almost four o'clock when the phone rang again. This time, it was Clarrise.

"She's back! She's back!" she shrieked into the phone. "I just left her! I just came home to get her some food," she said, " and now I'm going back." My heart leapt at the news. I had been slow to admit to myself, the disappointment I felt, but now let myself feel the flood of relief. I told her I would meet her there.

I gathered up Bandit (I knew Koko would be glad to see him, and it was almost walk-time), put him in his boots, and away we went. The high for the day of ten-below had come and gone and now the mercury was falling again. Twilight was creeping in and soon it would be dark.

We were like two mother hens, Clarrise and I, cackling over Koko, so glad we were to see her. She had no idea what the fuss was all about, and cared only for Bandit. She looked no worse for wear, though her feet were beginning to show signs of the exposure. She followed Bandit around the hill, sometimes hopping on three legs, her right-hind one off the ground, kicking at the empty air. I could only imagine what condition her pads were in. Soon her front feet were affected, and she limped back to her straw, to take refuge there. Clarrise placed a bowl of food next to her bed, which caused Koko to bolt from it. We moved away and she returned to gulp down the meal, keeping her eyes glued on us the whole time. She finished her meal and curled up in the straw, folding her legs and feet underneath as she dropped down. We stayed a respectful distance away. She seemed exhausted and wanting to rest. I thought we should leave: there was nothing more we could do. Clarrise said she would stay just a while longer. I hoped she would leave the animal be, and not cause her to roust from the straw.

I went home, satisfied that Koko would still be there come morning. She seemed intent to return to that place on the hill, for whatever reason. The temperature rose slightly during the night, as the clouds rolled in.

XIII.
The Sunday Visit

There was a fresh cover of snow when I went out the next morning, and it was still coming down. Bandit relished in the light, powdery stuff, rolling on his back from side to side and kicking his legs, making snow-angels. I couldn't help but join him. It was only ten-below, and with a light wind out of the south and a fresh blanket of snow for insulation, it seemed almost balmy. Like magic, the world had turned from a frozen wasteland into a real winter wonderland.

Koko was joyful to see us when we arrived at the hill. She got up and shook the accumulation of snow from her back. Her feet seemed to be doing better (helped out by the fresh fall of snow) and her spirits seemed brighter. She snatched a few wiener bites from my hand (I only had to crinkle the bag now, to summon her near) and frolicked around Bandit. We played the rope-game for a short while (I had stuffed it into my pocket on the way out), but with the snow still falling and a measurable amount already on the ground, I could see that Bandit was getting tired, so too soon, we were on our way. I knew he would be struggling, to climb the final hill to the car. He never gave in, he only slowed down. Koko followed us up to the lot, as had become her style.

I loaded Bandit into the backseat and stood beside the open door, trying to coax her in again, but I knew, it was to no avail. As Bandit was just ready to escape back out, I shut the door on him. "Gotta go, girl," I told her, "but you know, I'll be back." We pulled slowly from the parking lot, breaking trail through the several inches of new snow. I glanced back, for a final look at Koko, then did a double-take. She was following us! She was running desperately behind the car, in the tire tracks we made. I took a quick left, off of Thirty-sixth Street and onto Edmund Boulevard, the less busy of the two streets. (Though this early on a Sunday morning, and with conditions as they were, there wasn't bound to be much traffic.) I wasn't sure what to do next. I drove slowly, giving myself time to think and her, time to catch up. I really didn't think it was such a good idea, to have her follow me home this way, and then what? I decided to pull into the Dowling School parking lot, which was just around the corner.

I don't know who this person named Dowling was, but a lot of real estate had been set aside in his-or-her name. It used to be a school strictly for "handicapped" children, but now it was an open, public school. It sat on vast acreage, with the school building on the far eastern edge of the lot, facing Edmund Boulevard and overlooking the river. The grounds consisted of an orchard, a rolling field, a section of woods, a tree nursery in the far corner, and a section reserved for the gardeners in the summer, who could rent a plot at a nominal fee, to grow their vegetables and what-not. By crossing through Dowling at an angle from the river, you could emerge less than a block from our house, barely touching a residential street on the way. And this was the way I thought to bring Koko, if she was intent to follow, as she seemed to be.

I was excited at the prospect of bringing her home, but unsure of what to do once we got there. All of a sudden, things were happening too fast. I was not prepared for this development at all and was a little nervous, to be leading her so far away from (what she called) home. I left the car parked in the school's lot and we continued on foot. Bandit was having some trouble, forging through the deep snow, but he plowed ahead, always the trooper. Koko, with her long and striding legs, bounded effortlessly along, unabashed; that is, until we reached the far gate (which was really just an opening in the fence) that let out onto the street. This, she would not pass through. But with me calling to her and Bandit progressing away, she soon came along. She looked suspiciously at the houses that lined the street and the cars that were parked by the curb, staying a safe distance away from each. We made it into the alley and up to the back gate. I popped it open and herded Bandit into the yard. I followed him in, leaving the gate wide open.

"Come on, Koko," I called to her, and headed toward the house. Koko stood almost in the open gate, with her senses at full alert, surveying the area. With her head lowered and her feet planted firmly, she looked at me, then at Bandit, then at the gate; then at me, then at Bandit again. She inspected the gate up and down, and checked it from side to side. She hesitated to proceed. I went inside to rustle up a bowl of food for her.

Our backyard was bounded on both sides by a six-foot high, wooden privacy fence. The garage provided part of the boundary to the rear, with a four-foot high wire-mesh fence guarding the rest. The six-foot high stockade fence in the back gave way to a shorter wire-fence, about three feet high, that ran the length of the house, connecting to it at the front corner. It was a good yard for a dog. There was a lilac bush in one back corner and a tall, sheltering pine in the other; in the front quarter of the backyard, sat an enormous maple, which towered over the backyard and south side of the house, providing much needed shade in the summer.

I came out with the bowl of food, set it on the ground, and backed away. Koko watched my every move. Bandit stood by the house, looking on. Finally, she must have determined it was okay to enter, and cautiously stepped through the gate and into the yard. *If I can just get between her and the gate*, I thought. My heart was pounding. I didn't think the low fence in the front would be much of an obstacle for her, but I had to try. As Koko advanced slowly and further into the yard, I circled around behind her, nonchalantly. When the moment was right, I quickly side-stepped over and closed the gate. As soon as she heard the latch drop, her eyes went wild with panic. With her tail tucked down, she immediately turned and trotted toward the shorter fence in the front, as if she had already made some kind of plan. She hopped over it easily. Then she was out and in the street.

Now you've done it! I told myself, *she will never trust you again!* I ran out the back gate, securing it behind me (I didn't need *two* dogs on the loose), hoping to catch up to her out front, and then guide her back to the river. She wasn't safe here. I was afraid that she would either get lost (which is exactly what she was) or hit by a car. Koko met me at the entrance to the alley. Her eyes showed no ill-effect from the experience, but only looked at me as if to ask, now what?

"Now, I take you back to the river," I told her. So off we went, back through Dowling, this time leaving Bandit behind. She followed me anyway.

It was getting to be quite a chore, trudging through the deep snow, but I persevered; and it just kept falling. We passed by the car that I had abandoned earlier, on our way through the Dowling lot, and it was already covered. There was still very little traffic. We crossed the River Road and went down the few steps, to the lower path that would take us back to the hill. I broke trail down the path while Koko followed along in the trees. Once we arrived, I shook the snow out of her straw and fluffed it up.

"You gotta stay here!" I told her, trying to explain, but she just gave me a puzzled look. I turned my back on her and headed down the hill, but she was determined to follow. We stood in the valley and faced off. "No, Koko," I tried to be gentle but firm, but the message just wasn't getting across. "Get now!" I told her, a little more forcefully, and pointed back up the hill. It was of no use. I probably could have *scared* her away, with some flagrant word or action, but I didn't want to do that. I walked with her back up the hill. I stood near her straw, jumping up and down, trying to stay warm, wondering what to do next. My only hope was that someone would come along with a dog and distract her, long enough for me to make my getaway. But no one came.

I tried to leave again, but again, she followed me out. "Koko, you gotta stay!" I told her; I was beginning to get flustered. I started to back up the final hill, admonishing her all the way. "It's just too dangerous!" I was telling her. Then suddenly, she was distracted and her gaze shifted to the north. I took the opportunity to hurry up the last several yards and disappear over the top of the hill. Before I crossed the River Road, I checked to see if she was behind me. She wasn't. I felt a little guilty, for ditching her like that, but it had to be done. At least at the river, she was safe. It was what she knew.

XIV.
Build It, and She Will Come

I walked back to the car, alone in the thick silence of the new-fallen snow. My head was reeling from all that had occurred. I decided, it was probably a good thing, that she had followed me home, though we were no closer to actually catching her than we were before. Our fence was inadequate—that was as I feared—and there wasn't much to be done about it now, in the middle of the winter, with the ground all frozen and ice-covered. Even if we caught her, we couldn't keep her securely, and I was beginning to feel at a loss. Building a fence could be a major project, I knew that firsthand, and it wouldn't do to wait for the spring thaw. Something needed doing now. It looked like the noose or nothing. I decided to pursue it with a little more vigor.

Bandit was curled up in his straw, sleeping and all covered with snow when I arrived back. He looked cozy enough. He picked up his head and blinked the snowflakes away, looking at me wondering if it was walk-time again. "No, Bandit," I told him, and reinforced it by thrusting the palm of my hand toward him, which meant to him "stay." He tucked his nose resolutely back into his tail. I was exhausted from trekking through the deep snow. My legs felt drained and my toes were frozen. My face felt raw and the tips of my fingers were numb. I went in and stripped off my boots and gloves and plastered my hands and feet to the heater vent. My Sorels sorely needed new liners, I decided. I gritted my teeth against the fiery pain of thawing out. I lay on the floor and stared at the ceiling, listening to a song: James Taylor's "Walking Man," I think it was. I was anxious to tell Daniel about the new development. That was one thing about him being on the road that took some getting used to: there was no way for me to call him, I could only wait for him to call me; and he always did. Soon, the phone was ringing.

It was Clarrise. "I just got back from the hill, and I hate to say it, but she's gone again," she said, sounding dismayed.

"That's because she was here, at home with me!" I told her, maybe crowing a little, in my excitement. I explained to her how she had followed behind the car, and how I had led her back.

"Really!?" she said. "Isn't that interesting . . . ?" She sounded a little envious, but it wasn't a matter for that. I could almost hear the wheels turning inside her head. I told her that I thought it rather insignificant, as she had merely hopped over the fence, and we were no further along than before. "But that's good!" she insisted. "At least now she knows where you live!"

That didn't seem to matter either: I knew she would never venture here on her own. And that was good. Animal Control was often on patrol in the neighborhood, and though I knew they could never catch her, they did have their methods. And some members of the police force, it seemed, were none too fond of dogs, and took no chances when it came to strays. They had shot a man's wayward German shepherd, that had wandered into the downtown area. Seventeen times, I think. They said they thought it was a wolf. Then they had a snapshot taken of themselves standing around the lifeless animal, one with a rifle in his hand, and another standing with one foot propped up on the dead dog, in some kind of Big-Game Hunter pose. Unfortunately, the picture found its way onto the five o'clock news, and it made for some very bad publicity. The dog's owner eventually received a minor monetary award, for the property damage he sustained. So it was good that Koko stayed out of Dodge. She was no match for that kind of mentality. I could just envision her, standing on the edge of the hill against the tree-line, thinking she was safe, all wide-eyed and innocent, watching as the officer approached. She was fast, but not as fast as a flying bullet. She had no concept of that and would be a sitting duck. And if *she* sure didn't look like a wolf. . . . But for now, thankfully, it seemed she hadn't attracted the attention of the authorities. But I knew it wouldn't last forever. Someone was bound to turn her in eventually, and in that respect, the bitter cold temperatures worked in her favor: few people were out and about.

My mind wandered as I talked to Clarrise. She said that they had purchased a ton of cotton cord and were working on a net. Even as we spoke, Norman was tying knots. She thought it would take some time to complete, and a lot of knots, but Clarrise seemed to think that this was the way to go. She enlisted Daniel and me, each to man a corner, for the actual capture event. I had my doubts, and didn't commit to the project, but I didn't want to sound too discouraging either, for I had no fool-proof solution of my own to offer. But something about this plan worried me.

Clarrise said she was off to the hill, to see Soho, since she had missed her earlier that day and her dogs were ready for their morning outing. I said I would probably go later that afternoon, with the rope-toy. I told her what progress we were making with that. Koko was getting very careless of it, often allowing the rope to drag across her back, or prancing around with it draped over her shoulders. Sometimes, she would take the noose in her mouth, and with just the right flick of the wrist, I might have placed it securely around her neck. But it wasn't time for that—yet. I had abandoned the piece of plastic pipe for now, and had no desire to snare her *without* that buffer zone, fearing a negative reaction. It was true, Koko seemed to be a scared and harmless creature, but I didn't want to meet her evil twin. Clarrise said she had a muzzle I could borrow, just in case things went bad. I decided that that would be a good idea, and I would carry it in my pocket. I felt like the initiate, being sent off to the jungle to conquer the lion, with just the barest of tools and weapons for defense.

I knew inside that I would not even attempt to capture her, while I was there all by myself. Too many things could go wrong. I felt like I needed some backup, if only just for moral support. I didn't know what to expect, and it was this not-knowing that filled me with a nervous excitement and feeling of dread, each time we played tug-of-war and it looked like her head might slip through the noose. Not now, I would say to myself, not yet. And if I did catch her, did I expect her to walk calmly home beside me, like a domesticate on a leash? That was unlikely.

Snow kept falling throughout the day. The thick cloud cover helped boost the temperature to near zero. It was a welcome respite, all in all, except for the shoveling. Bandit lounged in the back corner of the yard, under the tall scraggly pine by the garage, keeping the squirrels in line. Daniel called. He had just crossed the line into Illinois, on his way back up.

Bandit and I had often accompanied Daniel in the big eighteen-wheeler. He was a very well-traveled dog. But as he got older, the road began to tell on him, and we were forced to stay behind. He was always eager to go, though he didn't cotton much to the actual traveling part, it was the getting there that he liked. He would always ride shotgun, stubbornly refusing to give up the passenger seat, watching for mile after mile, as the road disappeared under the big wheels. I rode mostly in the sleeper berth. It was a grand feeling, rolling down the highway, high above the four-wheelers, following the headlights down the neverending highway. Quiet, except for the hum of the engine. City-scapes would loom near, then disappear behind us, as we plunged headlong into the darkness. I had to hoist Bandit up into the cab to enter, and then to exit, he would take a leap of faith, into my open arms, and I would float him to the ground (we only missed once). He ate food from the can and drank water from the cooler. He was a good road-dog, and happy just to be along. But eventually, the stress of traveling got to be too much for him and we were grounded. Now I live vicariously through The Weather Channel.

I relayed to Daniel, the events of the day, and how Koko had followed us home. He was excited to hear it, even though she had escaped easily over the front corner of the fence. He wondered if I thought she might follow me home again. I assured him, she would. "Well!" he said simply, and a little too enthusiastically, "we'll just have to fix the fence!" I groaned: I knew that tone. I smelled a project coming.

Daniel had dragged me, kicking and screaming, into many a "project" over the years. He always claimed that there was "nothing to it!" and it would only take a couple of hours to complete—but I knew better. Ever the skeptic, I would see all of the complications before they arose, and would throw up roadblock after roadblock, begging myself out, knowing that it would take much longer and be a much bigger task than he was anticipating: he depended on me for this. But

Daniel's motto was, where there's a will, there's a way, and his first job was always to instill in me the will. Once that was done, and the project was begun, our idea of how a thing should proceed was always totally opposite. If I thought the nail should go in here, he thought it should go there; if I thought a one-by-two was sufficient, he was determined we needed a two-by-four; and so on, and so on, and so on. Our working relationship was tedious at best, and openly hostile at its worst. We tore down and raised a new garage a couple of summers before, both vowing we would be divorced before the project was finished (though we had never actually married). We laugh about it now, but one thing we learned was that if we put our heads and hands to work together, we could accomplish most anything. And once the job was complete, we would put our differences behind us and pat each other on the back, congratulating and complimenting ourselves for our cleverness.

To this idea, Daniel was committed: we would build a fence. Of course, he had no specifics, but he had plenty of time to think about it while he was driving. I had no doubt, he would come up with a plan. The project would commence when he returned the following day. I was encouraged by his enthusiasm, but held onto my doubt. I warned him about the new snow and the hazardous driving conditions, through Wisconsin and Minnesota. The winds were suppose to pick up and cause whiteout conditions by morning. "Don't drive with your eyes closed!" I gave him my usual admonishment. And then, "You be careful!" his admonishment to me.

XV.
The Clock is Ticking

Sometimes I ponder the question, suppose the season had been summer? Would this stray animal have commanded so much of my time? Or was she merely a distraction, a diversion, to relieve the boredom that comes with winter's bleak days and long nights? What if the conditions had not been so critical, would I have just let bygones be bygones, and given it no more thought than that? But it could have happened at no other time and in no other place. It was Synchronicity, pure and simple. Each condition was contingent on the next for its existence, and all of the conditions coalesced, in a specific time and place, to some dramatic end. Was I one of the contingencies? I certainly felt inexplicably drawn to her. She had attacked my conscience: I wanted to right the wrong that had been done to her, if a wrong there was. I wanted to be worthy of her trust and show her that she didn't have to go it alone; I would love and care for her. I was captivated and mystified by her and I know that other people felt it too, though each in their own, unique way. She invaded people's dreams. She was the host of a powerful spirit.

So it should be no surprise that I had increased my regular visits to twice-a-day. Bandit had to go out again in the afternoon anyway, and he really didn't mind the revisits to the river: it gave him a chance to "reclaim" his territory from the other dogs who had passed. Though he gave Koko little of his time (for that was his way), she didn't seem to mind, and greeted him always like a long, lost brother. Over the weekend, Clarrise and Norman had toted several bales of straw up to the hill and stacked them two-high, to create a three-sided shelter for her to use, to seek protection from the fierce winds. She seemed to prefer the bed out in the open though, probably finding the other too confining and enclosed, and with only the one way out. As I approached on the parkway, I could see the structure clearly through the trees, though I doubted if someone unaware would notice it.

I had the rope-toy with me, and a bowl of food. I hoped no one would be there, so we could concentrate more on getting used to the device. Very seldom, when I went to the hill, did Koko not have visitors. She had a regular stream of people and dogs coming through. Though no one knew just what to do about her, they enjoyed letting her play with their pets, getting them their exercise, with little output on the owner's part. She had become quite the novelty item.

There were several cars in the lot when I pulled in. It was a fairly nice Sunday afternoon, relatively speaking, with the temperature still hovering around zero, and people had come out of the woodwork. A woman and her two children were riding flying saucers down the steep hill from Koko's place; this was a popular sledding spot in the winter. As Bandit and I made our way down the first hill, the woman pointed up the next hill to where Koko was, and informed me that there was an animal up there, and it seemed to be *living* there. I let her know that I knew all about it, and holding out the bowl of food I was carrying, told her I had been feeding her. I assured her that the animal was perfectly harmless, in fact, she was quite frightened of people, and she wouldn't bother them. That seemed to put her at ease. She was wondering then, if she should contact Animal Control about it. I explained to her that we were in the process of befriending the animal, and were planning to take her home, and that calling Animal Control at this point was really not in the animal's best interest. She understood completely and even wished me "good-luck!" as we continued up the hill.

Koko was out of her straw and standing by the tree-line when we arrived. She seemed a little concerned over the appearance of so many people all of a sudden. I was a little surprised to see her actually, figuring with all the activity, she might have made herself scarce. Maybe she was getting a little *too* comfortable. I could almost hear the clock ticking over her head.

I shook the snow out of her straw and introduced her to the new look of the toy. I had threaded the rope back through the plastic pipe, with the noose on one end, and a large knot on the other. It was time to get serious. I left it to lay on the ground. She poked at it, inquisitively, with her nose. She wasn't too sure about its new and altered appearance, but eventually, took hold. The plastic pipe had a tendency to slide back and forth on the rope as we played, and I was careful to keep it from smacking her in the face. Soon, the game was under control, and she got used to the device and its unpredictability. Then, holding on to the very end of the pipe with my left hand, and grasping the big knot with my right, I held the thing out toward her as far as I could, dangling the noose right in front of her nose, daring her to take hold. She poked at it cautiously, and eventually did. I pulled the rope with my right hand, dragging it back through the pipe. She held fast to the loop, her eyes fixed on me intently. For a moment we stood there, stuck in time. If I could just flip the noose over her head, I would have her, I thought, *and* at arm's-length. But this was only a dress rehearsal—it wasn't time yet; but I knew, time was running out.

It had been a whole week, since I first met Koko, and neither I, nor anyone else, had been able to touch so much as a hair on her head. Her evasiveness was automatic and she could not be coerced. The only physical contact I had with her, was the stinging nip she gave my fingers, each time she snatched a treat from my hand. We had made little progress toward rescuing her, though there were several irons in the proverbial fire. She looked so worn and undernourished, and her right hind-foot continued to give her trouble. Her eyes looked tired and often held a silent, desperate plea. "It won't be long now, girl," I would tell her then, "and you'll be living like a queen! The Mississippi queen, that's what you'll be!" and offer what comfort I could.

She watched me crawl into the straw-bale shelter on all fours, turn around and lie down. I looked at the world through her eyes, gazing out from the enclosure. If she would just curl up and sleep here, I thought, but I doubted she would. Though it provided an excellent fortress against the elements, visibility was limited and hearing, impaired. But who could tell, when the night was at its deepest and most quiet, what play was rehearsed? Where did she go? What did she do? If only she could talk, imagine the stories she would have to tell! And I wondered how it all felt to her. Bandit stuck his nose in then, to investigate, snorted once, and lifted his leg on the bale of straw nearest the door, bringing me back to the moment. It really was time to go. We left Koko then, to curl up in her straw, with the twilight reaching down. The snow finally ended overnight.

Driving conditions were deplorable in the morning. The wind-driven snow piled drifts in the street. The sky was clear and the temperature stood at eleven-below, not too bad, but the wind was howling. We had received eight-and-a-half inches of new snow. I knew it would be a long haul for Bandit, but with the roads as they were, I thought we should walk to the river. Bandit was unaffected by the conditions and happy to be on his way. We walked the winding street, through the affluent neighborhood that sat between us and the river, keeping in the tire-tracks of the cars that had gone by. I knew that once we reached the lower path, we would be out of the wind. We made it up to the hill in good time. Koko greeted Bandit as usual, nuzzling him and throwing her big front paw over his shoulder. On her coat, she wore a thick blanket of ice; her whiskers and muzzle were heavy with it too. The wind-whipped snow stung her eyes and she squinted at me through the blizzard, disappearing and reappearing, as if in a cloud. This sucks! I thought. I had brought some dry dog food for her and laid the bag open near her straw. There was an empty can of Mighty Dog nearby. My main mission this morning was just to check on her, and having done that, with conditions as they were, there was little else to do but turn around and head home. I knew Bandit would be completely spent by the time we got there, though he was always anxious to go more, having no conception of his age-related limitations. Koko needed to follow.

It seemed that she longed for companionship, but there were so many obstacles in her way. I knew I couldn't dissuade her: if she wanted to follow, she would. I didn't like the idea, of her running around the neighborhood, but I would worry about that when we got to it. Right now, Bandit needed to head home. We made it across the River Road, Koko following cautiously along. She seemed to have a healthy respect for passing cars, though her strategy seemed risky. She would travel dead-center, down the middle of the street, an equal distance from the houses that lined either side (and the dangers that lurked there), watching ahead for approaching vehicles, her ears tuned behind. She was vigilant to know everything that was happening around her at all times; but when a lack of concentration and a vehicle collide, well, it would provide a sad end to the story. And there was always the x-factor, the random factor: the unexpected, the unpredictable. I knew it for a fact.

For part of my growing up, we lived in upstate New York, about thirty miles from the Canadian border. I had a dog named Keebler: "Keebie" I called him, for short. He was my best friend. He was a stray that had followed me home one day. He became a regular member of the family, along with our other dog, Koi (which was short for *koira*, the Finnish word for "dog"). I thought he had excellent car-sense, and would never meet his doom that way. Whenever he heard a car approaching, as he loped down the country road alongside me on my horse, he would head for the ditch. He stayed clear of the road as much as possible, and always looked before he crossed. But then there was the x-factor: the boy on the bike. That was the one thing Keebie couldn't resist. One day, he ran in pursuit and straight into the path of an oncoming car. I was away at college in Binghamton at the time, several hours away. My mother came down the following weekend to tell me the bad news; she brought his silver chain. (The way she tells the story is this: the accident had been less than an hour old, when out-of-the blue, on a sudden notion, I called from school, as if urged by a subtle sense of something wrong. "How's Keebie?" was one of my first questions. "Oh, he's fine," she assured me, "just fine," not wanting to tell me the real and tragic news over the phone; that is her rememberance of the event, anyway.) And a toy collie I had, when I was in grade school, met with a similar fate. So I was very apprehensive about Koko running around on the city streets.

But traffic was light and moving slowly, due to the conditions. Once we crossed the River Road and made it into the Dowling lot, I knew we would be safe. I let go of Bandit's leash. He was having a hard enough time in the deep snow, without having to drag me through it too. As we crossed the tree-lined median, between Edmund Boulevard and the River Road, Koko stopped and gazed into the sky. I looked up too. She was watching two crows, calling and circling overhead. I had never seen a dog take such an interest in birds before, and I thought it rather strange. When I turned again, to see how Bandit was progressing, I flipped into a mild panic. There was Koko, with Bandit's leash in her mouth, leading him back across the boulevard. She was taking him back to the river!

I went in hot pursuit. "No, Koko! No!" I shouted, trying to get there before they reached the busy River Road. (Bandit had no car-sense at all: one car on the road was too busy for him.) Bandit resisted, but they were on the way. "Bandit, stay!" I commanded, and he hesitated just long enough for me to catch up. When I got close enough, Koko dropped the leash. (This should have been a foreboding of things to come.) "Good boy!" I praised Bandit for waiting. Koko looked at me slyly. I held firmly to the leash as we continued our journey.

As we passed through the Dowling yard, Koko was distracted by a big, red rubber dodge-ball, left lying unattended in the snow. She grasped it between her incisors and carried it to the top of the nearest knoll, intent on its destruction. She deflated it easily, then shook it from side to side, slapping herself in the face severely several times. Then she would hold it on the ground with her two front paws and pull on it with her teeth; her neck and shoulder muscles bulged. It was over in a matter of minutes, and the shapeless piece of red rubber lay lifeless in the snow, forgotten. A golden retriever had appeared at the far gate, and Koko was off to play. I took the opportunity to hurry Bandit home, hoping to get back before she lost interest in the new friend, and then lead her safely back to the river.

Dowling was not a good place for her to be hanging out. There were signs that warned specifically, "keep dogs out," with the words spelled out in large capital letters, posted at every entrance, citing a specific children's playground ordinance number at the bottom, for added emphasis. And there *was* a playground here, but it was clear over on the other side of the grounds, toward the river, and fenced off separately from the rest and inaccessible. Technically, I didn't think this was a playground, and the signs, only the work of some virulent mind on an anti-dog campaign. Many people walked their dogs through here, and as long as they were in control, and the owners picked up after them, there was no reason for anyone to complain. That was my attitude, anyway. But Koko, running loose with no collar or tags, and looking decidedly wolf-like, it was reason for concern.

By the time I brought Bandit home and returned, the wind-blown snow had already filled in my tracks. I could feel every muscle in my legs working as I cut a new trail across the field, to where Koko was playing with the retriever. Luckily, I was naturally of an athletic build, and Bandit kept my walking legs in good tone, for I would need all of it to see me through this mission. I still had to return with Koko to the river and make my way back home. Even though Bandit wasn't along, I was confident she would take after me; we were beginning to develop some kind of rapport. Koko stood panting as I approached; her tongue was lolling and her eyes glowed with excitement.

"Is that the animal that's been living at the river?" the all bundled-up lady asked.

"Yeah, that's the one," I replied. Koko and Max, the retriever, had been having a good romp in the snow, equal in size and enthusiasm. "I'm going to get her back down there, too," I explained, "before the traffic gets any worse." We both agreed, this was not the best place for her to be. I headed down the middle of Dowling Street, walking in the tracks left by the car tires, beckoning for Koko to follow. She jumped at Max one final time, as if to say, gotta go!, then came bounding after me. She trotted along, a little behind me, and sometimes a little ahead, but never straying too far afield. (She was easier to keep track of than Bandit!) Once we crossed the parkway and made it to the path below, I felt we were safe, and relaxed. I stopped a minute, to catch my breath.

I leaned against the fence that bounded the cliff and looked across the river to Saint Paul. In the winter, with the trees bare, you could see the joggers and dog-walkers, way up high on the other side. They looked like little ants, scurrying along. The river far below looked frozen solid, covered with a fresh blanket of unblemished snow. I was glad that Koko showed no interest in crossing over. When it came to the river, looks could be deceiving. The ice was never safe but always static and changing. One day, the river might look frozen up solid, waiting for the Spring to be released, and by the next day, large, gaping holes of black, fast-moving water would appear. No, you just couldn't trust the river. Koko studied the movement across the way. She stood stone still; only her nose and ears twitched.

"Well, girl," I said, having rested long enough, "we best be on our way." And with that, we took up the last leg of the journey. As we crested the final hill, I saw Clarrise milling around the straw-bale shelter with her dogs. Koko raced ahead. "Hey!" I hailed her.

"Hey there!" she responded. "I thought she might be with you again!" she said. She went toward Koko, pointing and shaking her mittened hand at her saying, "I had a nice warm breakfast for you, but now it's frozen solid!" Koko backed away, eyeing her suspiciously. "Has she eaten anything this morning?" she asked. I told her that we hadn't made it all the way home, and as far as I knew, she hadn't.

"Well, I have a lamb and rice formula for her here, that should be easier on her digestion," Clarrise said. "Do you think you could keep her here, while I run home and throw it in the microwave? I only live a couple of blocks down Thirty-sixth." I told her I would do what I could, but since I was dog-less, I couldn't guarantee anything. I sat on a picnic table, with my chin in my hands, and watched Koko sniff around the field. She looked as if she could wander off any minute. Then someone arrived with a dog.

It was a tall, gray-haired man with a wire-haired terrier, named Thor. Thor and Koko appeared familiar with each other; they jumped and played. The man was friendly too, and soon we were in conversation. I told him what I had told countless others: we were willing to take the stray in, if only she could be had. He lived on Edmund Boulevard, and she had also followed him home on two separate occasions. He had fed her there, but had not been able to get her in anywhere. It was getting to be a common refrain. Soon, Clarrise had returned with the food. The gray-haired man and Thor left on their way.

Koko looked anxious to dine. She had worked up an appetite this morning, as had I. Clarrise set the food by Koko's bed and hovered near. Koko looked at the food and then at Clarrise. She paced a little, this way and that; then looked at the food, and again at Clarrise, who was either unconscious, or purposely teasing the animal.

"Maybe if you move away a little she'll eat," I suggested.

Clarrise began to taunt her. "What's a matter, baby-girl? Are you scared of me? Huh? Huh? Are you scared I'm going to reach out and *grab* you?" she said, making the motion with her hands. Koko looked uneasy and started to back away; I was feeling it too. But soon, Clarrise gave it up and backed off, allowing the animal to eat. I relaxed. As Koko ate, we talked. I began telling Clarrise about the day before, the woman and her two kids, and Animal Control.

"Oh, Animal Control knows she's here," she informed me. "In fact, the dog-catcher has been here a couple of times, looking for her, but luckily, she wasn't around at the time." This was news to me, and bad news indeed. I didn't know whether to believe it or not. But if it was true, and they were determined to locate her, and persistent (depending on how many complaints they received), eventually she would appear—and then disappear. The clock was ticking.

Our conversation turned to the topic at hand: how to catch her? The net was almost finished, Clarrise said, and would soon be ready for a trial run. I told her that Daniel was hatching a plan to heighten our fence, where it was too low. In effect, to create a large, live-animal trap out of our backyard. I urged her to hold off on the Daktari thing until we had a chance to try this approach. It seemed to be the most fail-safe and least traumatic of the ideas put forth so far, if it worked. Clarrise agreed, and said they would hold off with the net. I told her Daniel would be home anytime now, and we would start on it immediately. I predicted that we would have the fence finished by Tuesday, and by Wednesday morning, we could bring her home, early, before the traffic got started. She thought the plan had merit. I hoped Daniel had his thinking cap on because I hadn't a clue.

Clarrise offered me a lift home, which I gratefully accepted. It had been a long morning and Koko had already retired to her straw.

XVI.
The Trap is Set

We started on the project forthwith. Daniel was road weary, but energetic: he did some of his best work in that condition. The temperature had reached the afternoon high of twelve-below. The wind was brisk. I stood in the middle of the backyard, scratching my head, as Daniel laid out the plan.

We would have to block off access to the side yard. We would need to run a fence from where the six-foot fence ended, to the side of the house: a distance of about ten feet. Daniel, always on the far side of caution, thought it should be about eight feet high; I thought six would do. We would build a pre-fab structure, he decided, out of two-by-fours and the four-foot high, wire fence we had leftover from a previous project, and set it in the space. But how will we get it to stand there? I asked, ever the skeptic. The old asbestos, shake-siding was very brittle, and attaching anything to it directly was pretty much out of the question, unless we planned to re-side the whole house, come Spring. And the high wooden fence that bounded the backyard, was actually the property of our good-neighbors-to-the-south, and we couldn't really start pounding on that. Daniel was formulating a plan, ignoring my opposition.

We would need a piece of metal conduit, at least eight feet long, and just a bit smaller in diameter then the metal fence post that already stood there, just a few inches from where the privacy fence ended. We could drop the metal conduit down into the existing fence post, thereby raising it to the desired height. We would attach the end two-by-four, on the fence we were going to build, to the metal pole with plastic tie-wraps. (Daniel was a keen promoter of these handy little items, and found a zillion uses for them.) On the house-side, Daniel was puzzled, but soon came up with a solution.

There was a deep window-well surrounding the basement window, in just the right location. Daniel considered stacking two cinder blocks, down in the well, with the holes aligned and facing up. We would leave an extra length of two-by-four on that end of the fence, to drop into the hole, shim it up and fill it with sand. He was adamant that it would be sturdy enough to support the structure and hold it upright. (He had always been a firm believer in the properties of sand, for leveling and holding things in place.) Needless to say, I had my doubts. But it was too cold, and my head could not grasp any concept except for the fact of the sixty-below wind chill, and what were we even *doing* out here anyway? Daniel could see me floundering and took control. I relented.

We decided to work in the garage where we would be out of the wind; plus, we needed a large work surface for what Daniel had in mind. We backed the car out onto the cement slab. We decided to concentrate on the front section first, and worry about the back fence, where it was only four-feet high, later.

Daniel worked as if driven to it. He was pursuing a vision. Totally out of character for myself, I stood aside and let him work, offering my assistance where I could. Besides, it was just too cold to argue. Much of the job had to be done with gloves removed, and it didn't take long before our fingers were frozen and clumsy. (In these severe temps, exposed flesh could freeze in a matter of a minute; I wondered what that ratio was, when exposed *and* in contact with bare metal?) When we couldn't stand it anymore, we would run for the house, to wrap our numbed fingers around steaming cups of coffee. We pulled off our boots and rubbed our toes, to get the circulation flowing again. Then out we would go again, to resume the chore. Daniel was confident and strong in his resolve; I only hoped that our effort would not be in vain.

First, we made a frame out of two-by-fours, seven feet high and ten-feet long. We added braces and cross-braces for strength. We stapled the four-foot wire fence to the frame, twice high. It was a sturdy and impressive structure, indeed. Now, if we could just fasten it securely in place, between the house and fence, phase one of our task would be complete. But that would have to wait until morning. It was getting late, and almost time for Bandit's walk. Soon, it would be dark. We carried the structure into the backyard and leaned it against the fence: the car would be requiring the garage tonight.

We decided to gear up and head for the hill. Daniel hadn't seen Koko since his return. It had been a brutal day, weather-wise, and I wanted to see how she was getting along. We prepared a warm meal.

We were greeted by an ominous sight when we reached the hill that afternoon: there were fresh tire-tracks in the snow, leaving the parking lot, over the curb. We followed them down the first hill and up the second. A vehicle had been to the very place where Koko made her bed. The tracks continued down the far side of the hill and disappeared. Several things raced through my mind: had Animal Control finally come for her? Koko was nowhere in sight. Maybe it was just a park-maintenance vehicle, or the Park Patrol. It might have been the cops. Whoever it was, they were obviously authorized to drive on park property, which made them (in some way, shape, or form), the Authorities—and in this event, the enemy. The situation grew immediately more urgent.

I looked out across the river and let out a shrill whistle, hoping to roust Koko. I studied the land below for any sign of movement, but the wind driven snow made visibility poor. I whistled and called again. Daniel walked to the other end of the hill, scouring the hillside. But there was nothing. I was getting a little worried. Then Daniel called to me from the other side of the picnic ground, "Turn around! Look behind you!" I turned, and there she was, standing no more than three feet away, looking up at me calmly.

"There you are!" I exclaimed, a little startled by her sudden appearance, though totally relieved I was. She had probably been scared off by the vehicle. And even though *she* might have escaped notice, the straw-bale fortress and the big pile of it, that sat dead-center in the middle of the field, was a sure giveaway that some subterfuge was going on here. I was sure, that whoever had made the tracks, would be back to investigate. Koko retreated immediately to her straw. She was cold and tired. I approached to place the bowl of food nearby. She bolted from the straw.

"Oh, Koko," I implored her, "you don't have to run away from me. I would *never* hurt you," but I knew that all the talk in the world would never convince her of that. It was a reflex action and out of her control. We left her lying in the straw, with her nose tucked deep into her tail. She looked so lost and forlorn. I promised her that we would be back, first thing in the morning. If she could just survive another night.

"Another cold snap is on the way!" the television screamed at me. The Alberta Clipper was coming at us, heading in out of Canada. I must have missed the "warm snap" I mused: it must have been that brief moment yesterday, when the temperature made it all the way up to zero. Strong winds and twenty-six below temps would combine to create wind chills in the seventy-five to eighty-below range, the forecaster said, advising us about wind chill dangers and exposed skin, and that any outdoor animals should be brought inside. (Hah! I thought.) Also, whiteout conditions again by morning, with blowing and drifting snow. How could Koko possibly survive *this*? I wondered. We would tackle the fence, first thing in the morning. I cursed the cold and the dark.

That night, I dreamed that the dog-catcher was combing the streets of South Minneapolis, searching for Koko. As the Animal Control truck passed by, I looked at the driver and he looked at me: I knew that face! It was the guy who had prepared our Subway sandwiches, earlier that day! I awoke then, confounded by the absurdity of the dream, thinking what a mind, to play such a hoax! Then my head was filled with Koko. Had she survived another frigid night, the worst so far? I was anxious to know. The day was still dark, but beginning to dawn.

Koko was still alive and kicking when we arrived at the hill the next morning, apprehensive though she was, to leave her straw and the warm nest she had created. She rose reluctantly and stretched; her coat was laden with ice and icicles hung from her chin. She tried to work up some enthusiasm, seeing Bandit, but soon retreated to her straw, limping badly on three legs; her feet were totally gone. It was pathetic. Out of sheer desperation, I tried repeatedly to approach her straw, but each time, she bolted from it. It was useless. The best thing we could do was let her lie, and return home to work on the fence. The situation had become ever more critical; the weather, our unyielding adversary.

That day produced the coldest high on record, sixteen-below. It was relentless, and it got even worse.

Daniel's plan to use the cinder blocks in the window-well worked without a hitch. The wind chill, now only fifty to sixty-below, was commonplace, and an improvement over the eighty-below, that had been overnight. We worked silently and with purpose. We decided on a simple solution for heightening the fence in the back: we had some leftover four-by-eight sheets of waferboard, from when we had built the garage. We cut them to size and screwed them into the wooden posts there, raising its height to nearly six feet. It was ugly, but it worked. We did the same thing to the gate, but had to do it in such a way, that the gate would still function. You could still see through the fence at the bottom, where it was wire, from a dog's-eye view; the waferboard started about two feet up. By nightfall, the job was complete. The trap was set.

I went alone that evening, to visit Koko. It was dark out and already twenty-below. The inside of my nose burned with every breath I took. The quarter moon shone bright in the clear sky. Ice crystals sparkled and filled the night air; the wind had abated for the moment. Koko sat up and stretched as I approached. She jumped from the straw as I placed the bowl of food near the edge of her bed. I retreated quickly.

"It's alright, girl," I assured her. "You sit in that bed and I'll just sit over here, in this one," I said, and crawled into the straw-bale shelter and leaned against the back wall, facing out. Koko went back to her straw. We sat there together in the cold silence, for what seemed like a timeless period. She was aware of my company, though I don't know what solace it provided. But before long, I was chilled to the bone: my body convulsed uncontrollably and my teeth were chattering. I had to leave. I offered her what words of encouragement I could, but I knew she needed much more than that, to see her through this night. I said a silent prayer to the stars up above. What was the significance of this experience in the arena of the whole universe? I wondered. Then I walked back to the car in the sullen light of the moon, leaving her to face another long and bitter-cold night alone. It was all I could do.

"Record breaking lows for tonight!" the man on the tv crowed, "with temperatures near thirty-five below!" He seemed to be getting some perverse pleasure out of announcing it. My heart sank. I wanted to throw something through the tv screen, but I knew it wouldn't change the awful fact. I just turned it off; I had heard enough. I felt helpless and was beginning to feel quite hopeless. Could it get any worse? Even though the fence was ready and finished, there was no way Koko could make it here, in these temps. Her feet were severely compromised already, and I was afraid any further punishment would result in permanent and irreparable damage. We would have to wait: the Alberta Clipper was notorious for moving through quickly. The conditions just *had* to get better; they sure couldn't get much worse. I wasn't too concerned about the authority-factor for now: only a fool would be out looking for an elusive, stray dog in this weather, and certainly, not any of the city's employ. Our mission for now would be just to keep her alive, until the time was ripe.

The next day, Koko was nowhere to be found. I wasn't too concerned. The bitter-cold had sent her off, I surmised, to wherever it was she went when the arctic winds blew at their worst. I imagined she had a special perch, where the very first rays of sun hit and lapped warmly against her fur. I expected her to appear, as the sun rose higher in the sky. By early that afternoon she was back. That day, the temperature rose to above zero for the first time in a week: it made it to one.

Things were looking up. Koko had regained her cheerful composure and jumped and poked at Bandit. Daniel and I sat on a straw bale and watched. Koko approached near. She kept one eye on us as she gnawed through the twine that held one of the bales together. It *popped!* as it broke and she playfully jumped away. "Koko," I admonished her, teasing. "What the heck are you doing?" She studied me carefully as she went to work on the second twine. She chewed through it easily, and the bale fell apart. She jumped into the middle of the loose sheaves and began, joyfully and frantically, clawing and biting, throwing straw everywhere, looking toward us, she appeared to be laughing. And so were we. I fell off the bale of straw where I had been seated, totally regaled. Then she was ready for a chase. I pursued her and she pursued me, ducking and dodging behind the trees. The temperature was right, but it was too late in the day to bring her home. But she was in good spirits, and that was at least half of the battle.

I was in awe of her, I have to admit. I knew we were proceeding toward some end, but the prospect of actually obtaining her had somehow passed me by. Sooner, I could pluck a star from the sky. I almost expected her to disappear at any moment, in a *poof!* of smoke, leaving us to wonder what *that* had been all about, or if it had even happened.

When we returned again later that afternoon, Koko and I played the rope-game. We had pretty much abandoned this approach, in favor of the large live-animal trap, but Koko still liked the sport of it. As we played, all of a sudden, the rope came in a perfect position to become a noose around her neck! "Daniel!" I whispered, in a hushed and dramatic tone, "I think I can get her. I *know* I can!" My knees felt weak. "What should I do?" The moment of decision was upon me.

"No!" Daniel advised me, "let it be! Tomorrow. The fence is finished. We'll take her tomorrow. It's the best way; and it's the safest way. Just one more night!" I relaxed then, thankful to him and his decisiveness. I knew he was right. Suddenly, the event soon to occur became all too real.

XVII.
The Trap is Sprung

I slept fitfully that night, my head full of the possibilities, the ifs and what-ifs. I woke up every hour and looked at the clock. I tossed and I turned; my stomach was in knots and my head was spinning. When the alarm sounded at four a.m. I felt as if I hadn't slept at all. It was still the middle of the night. I dragged myself out of bed and started the coffee. I was operating on automatic pilot. I got some kind of demented pleasure out of driving myself to exhaustion (and even a little beyond), and in the mental state that was achieved; and it was certainly upon me this day.

Daniel got up, optimistic and energetic. "Today's the day!" he crowed, trying to arouse some enthusiasm. I groaned. The wind howled outside, and the windows rattled ominously. It would be my best night's sleep for a long time to come, but I had no idea of that at the time.

We didn't talk much as we drank our coffee (the perfect tonic for an already upset stomach). "I just hope she's there," was about all I could say. We had laid out our plan the night before. We would arrive at the hill by five. That would give us plenty of time to lure her home, in the quiet morning, before the hustle and bustle, providing for fewer distractions and a safe journey. Bandit would have to come: he was the bait; she was our quarry. I was confident she would follow the car, as she had before. We would drive slowly and park in the Dowling lot, and walk the rest of the way. Daniel would go back later, to retrieve the car. At least, that is how we had it planned.

The sky was still black when we left the house. We were way ahead of Bandit's schedule, and he was a little confused, but once we convinced him that he really *could* come along, he responded with his usual exuberance. I struggled to put him in boots and harness. The mercury held steady at sixteen-below; though still bitter-cold, it *was* an improvement. I hoped Koko's feet would hold up. I fixed her favorite treat, bite-sized pieces of wiener. It was illegal to park in the river lot before six a.m. so, not wanting to attract any attention, we left the car on Edmund Boulevard and walked across the River Road. Then proceeded down the hill. It was kind of spooky out; I felt like the proverbial thief that comes in the night. Something didn't feel quite right.

When we reached the hill, Koko was nowhere around. I whistled and called; we stood and listened. We were too early. We waited some more but she didn't show. The whole thing was very anti-climatic. I was almost grateful for her absence, reluctant to get the thing under way. We decided to go home and warm up, then return again in forty-five minutes or so.

The sky had still not begun to lighten, when we returned. Still, there was no sign of her. Daniel stood on the edge of the hill and gave the special call that he had developed: "Coo-coo to Koko!" he chortled into the darkness and out across the river. "Coo-coo to Koko!" for we surely thought ourselves nuts. She didn't respond. We left, only to return again later.

It was almost six-thirty when we got back, and still an hour before dawn. Bandit stayed home this time: I didn't want to put him through another dry run; his stamina was waning, and we might need his strength later. We could race home to retrieve him, if necessary. Koko was nowhere around. We called and listened and waited. I was getting anxious and cold. I went to the deep glen, below and to the north of the hill, to peer over the fence there, where she might come up, and called some more. No response.

"I don't know, what do you think?" I called up to Daniel.

"I think you should turn around and look behind you!" he said, always the smart-alec. This time I knew what to expect. Koko had snuck up on me silently, in the dark, and was standing no more than an arm's-length away.

"Damn-you, Koko," I said. She looked a little offended. She followed me up to the top. I offered her a wiener treat, but she wanted nothing to do with it. She brushed right by me, disinterested, and headed directly for her straw; I could see, she wasn't going anywhere. She was breathing hard from exertion, and her whiskers and muzzle were coated with frost. She looked totally done-in. She rose a couple of times and went to look nervously over the side of the cliff, each time, returning to her straw. What was going on down there? I wondered; something had her on edge. We tried to get her to follow us, coaxing her with the treats, but she wouldn't cooperate. She stayed staring at us from her straw. We decided to let her rest awhile, then return once more, with Bandit; he was our ace-in-the-hole. The hour was getting late.

It was light out by the time we returned to the hill for the fourth time that morning, a little after eight. Bandit was rested and ready to go. We pulled up in the lot, beside a large, white van: it was some kind of parks-and-recreation vehicle. I wondered what they were up to. We looked at each other, and not saying a word, made haste. We scrambled down the first hill and up the next. We were confronted by three workmen, in work clothes and wearing hard-hats: one was toting a chainsaw, one had a long pole (which looked like the snare-device used by Animal Control, but was really just something for cutting limbs), and the third, I don't remember. They were looking at Koko, who was sitting still, on the far edge of the clearing, looking at them.

"What are you going to do," I challenged them, "cut her head off?" I don't know why I said it, but that is really what I said. My only excuse is that my nerves were frazzled and I was feeling very defensive.

They looked at me curiously, and said harmlessly, "Boy! That sure looks like a wolf, doesn't it?" We briefly told them her story, and said we were about to take her home with us, right now. We strode deliberately to the other side of the hill and called to her.

"Come on!" Daniel urged me in a low voice. "We have to do it now! Let's go! Get moving!"

I became immobilized: my legs would not move. I was filled with apprehension. Now that the moment was upon us, I choked. "But . . . but . . . ," I stammered.

"Let's go!" Daniel's voice was firm. "What's the matter with you?" Finally I found my legs and we proceeded. "Come on, Koko! Come on Bandit! Come on!" Daniel herded us away and down the path. As we traveled down the lower path to Thirty-eighth Street, where we could cross, Daniel took up the lead, with Bandit and then me in the middle, and Koko trailing along behind. We were on our way. Not according to plan, we would walk the whole way home.

The traffic was heavy on the River Road by that time. Often, the wait for a break in it could be a long one, but miraculously, as we approached, the traffic cleared.

"Come on!" Daniel said, still prodding us along, "hurry up!" I walked as if in a trance.

My thoughts raced ahead to what would happen, once we got home. Would she even come in the yard? Maybe she remembered from the time before. Would we be able to get her in far enough to close the gate? She might be savvy to that. And if we did, then what? But the matter at hand, was to get there. We came up with an impromptu plan.

Once we got into Dowling, I would race ahead and open the back gate, grab the bowl of food from the kitchen and set it out on the garbage cart, in the alley. Daniel would lag behind with Bandit and Koko. Then I would run back and meet up with them, before they left Dowling. I would take Bandit and Daniel would race on ahead, to take up his position, in the garage. Once I coaxed Koko far enough into the yard, Daniel would slide out from his hiding place, and shut the gate behind her. Timing was everything: he musn't be too eager, or reticent either; I didn't envy him, his position.

As we traveled through the Dowling lot, a loud voice interrupted our plan-making: it was the man who shouted commands at his two black labs, that we had met previously, at the river. "Oh, great . . . ," Daniel moaned. He was afraid Koko would be scared off by the loud voice, or distracted by the dogs. But I knew she was familiar with them, and though she drifted in their direction, I was confident she would take up again, behind Bandit; which she did. Finally, we were in the Dowling yard.

"Run now!" Daniel commanded me, "run!" I started out at a brisk jog, heading for home. Daniel's voice echoed behind. "Run!" he said, "and hurry back!" It took every ounce of energy I had, to jog through the snow on the uneven path through the orchard. When I emerged onto the street, I stopped to catch my breath. "Run!" I heard Daniel's voice behind me; they were catching up. I cursed him silently under my breath, then jogged on. I got home and made the preparations.

By the time I made my way back, the troupe had already reached the corner. Daniel handed Bandit off to me and went on ahead, to assume his hiding place, in the garage. I told him to make sure and prop the gate open, with the rock, or it could swing shut at the most inappropriate time. "I know, I know," he assured me, focusing on his task at hand. Everything was clicking into place. The tension kept mounting, the closer we got. I wondered if Koko could sense the nervousness and anticipation.

She followed us home, but approached the gate warily. I picked up the bowl of food and carried it into the yard. Koko watched with interest, but was very suspicious. Her nose perked up a little. We had made her a bed of straw in the middle of the yard, and I walked toward it.

"Come on in, Koko," I beckoned to her. My voice sounded steady and calm, but my insides were jumping up and down. I looked at the door to the garage; it was cracked ever so slightly. I could feel Daniel there, watching. I left the food by the straw and walked over to pet Bandit, who was standing near the back door. "See, Koko," I said, "I like a dog!" I cooed and fawned over Bandit, ignoring her altogether, but watching out of the corner of my eye. She advanced further into the yard. I looked at the garage door, trying to send Daniel a telepathic message: Now! I screamed inside, do it *now*! But the door never budged. Koko took a few more steps into the yard. Suddenly, the door opened and Daniel slipped out. He went quickly, and calmly closed the gate.

Koko bolted toward the front, where she had escaped before, but the way was blocked. She ran frantically toward the back fence, but it was too high. I moved toward her steadily with the rope (that was always in my pocket) in my hand.

"It's okay, girl, " I tried to soothe her, "we're just trying to help you." I had her cornered between the lilac bush and the back fence: and that is where she surrendered herself to me. I slipped the heavy rope over her head and around her neck. It was over.

I thought I had prepared myself for every eventuality, when this final moment came, but I was not at all prepared for what actually did happen. Nothing. Koko stood motionless, and the light went out of her eyes.

PART TWO

XVIII.
The Cave

It is hard to describe exactly how it felt, when that final moment came. I was overwhelmed by a plethora of conflicting emotions. There was a vast sense of relief, but also, a sense of trepidation. I felt exhilarated and deflated, all at once. My victory was her defeat. It was a fragile moment.

"Daniel," I spoke, trying to keep my voice calm and light, "could you get me the gray, nylon choke-collar from the house, and a leash?" He went to retrieve the items. For the first time, I reached out and stroked her ever-so-lightly on the right shoulder. She really was real! "Everything is going to be okay, now," I told her, then withdrew my hand. I was mindful not to handle her too much; events had been traumatic enough, and I could tell that she thought my touch very strange. At least the days of standing out in the below-zero temps and bitter-cold winds were over, the agonizing over her condition, the feelings of helplessness and frustration; that's what I thought, anyway.

Daniel brought the collar and leash. He made his movements slow and deliberate. I gently slipped the collar over her head and removed the thick rope from around her neck. Koko showed no reaction. Her eyes stared off, lifelessly. She was in a state of total surrender and ready to accept her fate, which was now in my hands. I did not take the responsibility lightly.

"Come on, Koko," I said, gently tugging on the leash, coaxing her to walk with me. She came along easily and without regard. I gave her plenty of slack: I wanted to see if she would have a try at the fence. I'm sure she was as curious as I was, to see if our fortress was strong. It didn't take long to find out. From a complete standstill, Koko jumped straight up into the air and hooked her front legs over the waferboard barricade we had erected. She pedaled furiously with her back feet, trying to pull herself over. She would have succeeded too, had I not foiled her attempt. I pulled on the leash with just enough force to bring her back to the ground.

"No, Koko, no," I admonished her gently, "stay down!" She stood staring off into space. I persuaded her to walk with me again. Bandit stood several feet away, watching as the action transpired. Every so often he emitted a series of barks, to voice his excitement or displeasure. He wasn't sure if he liked this stranger, being in his yard. (He would forever wait for Koko to go home, like Katie-the-dog did, after Christmas.) He tolerated her only because he thought she would be leaving soon. And it was ironic, because without *him*, there would be no *her*: he was the key that had unlocked the door.

Koko and I traveled the perimeter of the yard, searching for other weak spots. I think she could have gone over just about anywhere, given enough time and distance, to achieve the proper momentum, for she certainly had the motivation, but the main vulnerability seemed to be in the rear. It was a disheartening realization. I would have to keep her on a leash for now. We just couldn't risk losing her, for her sake, as well as ours. And I would not have her, tied.

I would rather have no dog at all, than one that had to be imprisoned in a kennel or confined to a chain, to live out its days like that. (I had purchased a heavy-duty chain, for just that purpose, just in case, and secured it to the bottom of the washpole, where it lay now, cold and lifeless, forgotten in the snow.) No, she would have to come to accept this as her home, and us, as her pack. Only then would she stay. It had to be of her own volition. There would be no cages or chains: the bonds that held her would be intangible. But it would take time.

I wanted to let Clarrise know we had her. I knew she was eager to hear, and was probably on pins and needles, waiting by the phone. After all, she was our co-conspirator and had put forth a lot of time and effort, in the animal's behalf. Besides, I needed to tell someone!

Daniel took the leash from me and he and Koko continued the tour of the yard. It was still near fifteen-below.

"Better stay clear of that back fence!" I warned him.

"Don't worry!" he replied, "you bet I will!" He handled her as if she was the most fragile flower, ever so gently, and caressing was his tone. I went in to use the phone.

"Well, we got her!" I told Clarrise, triumphantly, and wondered if she could hear the underlying nervousness in my voice.

"You have her!?" she squealed, in disbelief. "Can I come see her?" she asked.

"You bet!" I said. "We'll be out in back. I'll leave the front door unlocked and you can just come on through." She was over in a matter of minutes.

I let her walk Koko around the yard a little. She tried to pull Koko to her, so she could touch her. Koko resisted, but she was persistent. I watched them unconsciously, as if in a dream. Clarrise led Koko a little too close to the back fence. Koko jumped up and hooked her legs over, as she had done before, and tried frantically to pull herself over; Clarrise stood by, unaffected. She's going over! I thought, and snapped out of my trance. I made a move forward, to intervene, but at the deciding moment, Clarrise jerked down on the leash and Koko fell to the pavement, on her back, with a thud.

"Wow!" Clarrise exclaimed, "did you see that? She almost went over!" I took the leash back.

I thought it was time to find Koko a place to be. I needed to go inside and warm up. It had been a long morning since four o'clock, and a long time out in the cold. I didn't think the animal would feel at all comfortable in the house and I was fearful at the damage she might do there, being so unfamiliar with it and all. The garage seemed to be the most obvious choice; at least to confine her there temporarily and get her out of the elements, while we went inside to warm up and regroup. I was kind of surprised when I walked into the garage with Koko, to see it vacant—I had completely forgotten about the car we had left at the river. I fluffed out some straw for her in the back corner, behind the motorcycles (which stood covered-up for the winter). I removed the leash and backed out of the garage. She tried to follow. I hated to leave her, shut in there like that, but it was all I had at the moment. The door closed in her face with a heavy thud.

We sat at the kitchen table and gave Clarrise a detailed account of the events as they had occurred, talking over and interrupting each other excitedly, as we built up the suspense to the final moment. Daniel went repeatedly to the garage to check on Koko, standing on a stump to peer in through the high window. He reported that she was very ill-at-ease and was searching desperately for a way out. She had been up on the workbench and had knocked several things to the floor, and we would notice later, she had grabbed a hold of and pulled on the wiring that ran along the top sill of the garage. Luckily, she hadn't bitten it through. There were too many things out there she could get into or hurt herself on, I was afraid, and though not hastened to do it, she desperately needed the warmth of the house; I decided to bring her inside. I expected her to feel very claustrophobic and intimidated, and asked Daniel and Clarrise to remove themselves to the front of the house, into the living room. I would go and get her and bring her in on a leash, in case she got berserk.

Koko shied away as I entered the garage. She ducked and dodged me for awhile, but eventually I got her cornered and was able to reach out for her collar. She crouched in terror; her eyes were wild with fear. I took hold of her gently and snapped the leash onto her collar.

"Don't worry girl, I'm not going to hurt you," I soothed. "I just want to get you someplace warm." The freezing concrete was beginning to affect her feet. Once the leash was on, she was as submissive and docile as you could want. I led her to the house. By now, Bandit was up and coming. "Come inside, Bandit," I motioned him toward the house, which immediately sent him back, to curl up in his straw. I dragged Koko in the back door ahead of me.

As soon as we got inside, Koko assumed a crouching position. With her tail plastered tightly between her legs, she was off. She searched through the house, her nose barely an inch off the ground, taking in all the smells, her eyes glancing furtively, every which way. She investigated every corner, every room, every nook and cranny. Soon she had pulled me back through the kitchen and we were headed down the basement stairs. And there the process of discovery began again. When she got to the dark place, under the basement stairs, she explored it briefly, then abruptly, lay down: she had chosen.

The space under the basement stairs was partially blocked off by a workbench. The distance between it and the basement wall, was about a foot-and-a-half, and it formed a perfect door to the dark place underneath. I couldn't have picked a better spot myself! It was perfect: warm (but not too) and secluded. I squatted down to remove the leash. "There you are, girl," I told her. "See! It's not so bad." I was careful not to loom over her and appear threatening, although by my very human being-ness, I was. I went back upstairs to report.

"Well, she found her spot!" I said. "Her very own, personal, indoor cave, right under the basement stairs!" It was more than I had hoped for. We all expressed our delight. The animal was finally in, and her fate seemed secure. Everything would be all right. She wasn't violent at all, only fearful and docile. She had shown not the slightest hint of aggression, only total submission. I thought things were going rather well.

Daniel still had to go and recover the car. Clarrise offered him a lift, but he declined. A good brisk walk was just what he needed to relieve his mind and the pent-up energy left in his body; he bundled up and set off. Clarrise stayed a while longer. I told her to bring Norman by later, if he wanted to visit the captive, as he had also put forth a lot of time and effort for the animal's well-being, and it seemed only right. He was the complete opposite of Clarrise, shy and introverted. He shunned contact and conversation, and ours had been only limited. He would not speak unless spoken to directly, then he would avert his eyes as he talked. I felt awkward around him, never knowing quite what to say, but he was welcome to come and see the animal. I had no intention of keeping her selfishly to myself. He had every right.

When Daniel eventually returned with the car, Koko still had not budged from her cave. I hadn't heard a peep out of her. She seemed to be content to stay there, and showed no inclination toward moving. We decided it would be safe to leave her alone for awhile. We were anxious to supply her with the items that our new addition to the family would need: her own dog bowl, collar and leash, and other sundries, to legitimize her acceptance here.

We decided on special precautions to insure her safety, and the safety of our "stuff." We would have to leave Bandit inside, because of the conditions, but we would close the kitchen door, at the top of the basement stairs. She could come up to the landing and to the back door, but wouldn't have access to the house. I made sure Bandit was settled and the coffee pot was turned off and we left, totally forgetting to close the basement door. We were off in search of that very special gift, for that *very* special dog.

Daniel insisted that the first thing we needed to get was a name tag. The message would be the same as the one on Bandit's: the dog's name, telephone number (with area code), and the word "reward" spelled out in large, capital letters. It seemed rather superfluous to me. I knew no one would ever get close enough to her to read it, unless of course, she was dead, and then I would rather not know. But Daniel was staunch on this, and he was right. We would get her a tag.

Bandit seldom wore his collar now, when he was in the yard. It seemed like such a small freedom to grant, like removing your tie at the end of the day. And now that his wanderlust was so tempered with age, he was easy to keep track of and would totally ignore an open gate, showing no inclination whatsoever to escape. A far cry from his younger years, when the slightest breech in security could prove costly. But for awhile, we would be back on a heightened-security-alert. And we knew the drill well; all gates would be kept locked.

We returned home to find that we had left the door to the kitchen wide open. "Oops!" I said sheepishly, like the child who has spilled the milk, but my fears were unwarranted: nothing had been disturbed. Koko had not stirred from the basement. I went to check on her.

It was very dark in the basement. The only dim light came from one small window, up in the front, on the north wall; the others had been boarded over by the previous owners. (We had been homeowners here, for less than three years.) I reached overhead and pulled on the light-chain, to light the bare bulb. It was high and off to the side and did not shine directly on her, but cast enough light that way for me to see her there, lying in the shadows. She hadn't touched the food or water I had placed earlier, near the entrance to her cave. She lay pasted against the back wall on her belly, with her rump pressed tightly in the corner and her front legs forward; her chin was tucked into her chest. She looked at me with wide and innocent eyes that held a profound sadness. She was so beautiful! As I approached closer, she rolled onto her side and lifted her hind leg, in a gesture of pure submission.

"Oh, Koko," I implored her, "it doesn't have to be that way." My eyes filled with tears, as I was filled with compassion. And her vulnerability aroused in me a fierce sense of protectiveness. "No one will ever hurt you again," I pledged to her, "I promise." And I *did* mean it, with every fiber of my being. I crawled up to her carefully, and stroked lightly, her exposed belly. She seemed to relax a degree, but continued to lay motionless; her eyes stared vacantly ahead to the darkest place under the stairs. I thought it best to leave her be for now. It had been a long day for her too, and her life was in total upheaval.

I turned off the light then, and left her, alone in the dark again. But this time she was safe and warm, and I glowed with the satisfaction of knowing that. And there she stayed and collapsed, for two nights and two days.

XIX.
Silent Night

That night we were in a celebratory mood. Daniel prepared for us a feast of baked chicken and Stove Top Stuffing Instead of Potatoes. For the first time in many days, I felt a sense of peacefulness and contentment, though shrouded somewhat, by a deep sense of commitment. But it no longer mattered to me, how low the temperature dropped, or how hard the winds blew. There would be no more trips to the river, in unbearable conditions. A great weight had been lifted (though another soon would fall). But for now, we basked in the glory of our accomplishment. It was a gratifying feeling to know she was there, in safety and warmth, one floor below. Against all odds, the rescue had been a success; it was hard to believe.

Bandit received a generous portion of chicken that night, a reward for his part in the endeavor. He had been a real trooper, as usual, unstoppable and single-minded he was, keeping pace through the cumbersome snow, in ungodly temps, as if he had some greater purpose in mind. It took all he had and then some, but he never faltered once; he had performed his part superbly. I hugged him extra tight and smothered him with kisses, grateful for him and his magnanimity. We ate heartily that night, full of appetite. The mood was jubilant and light. Clarrise and Norman would be by later, to see Koko.

"I bet Koko would like some chicken," I said, and we headed downstairs with our offering. She lay as before, but with her neck lowered and outstretched, and her chin barely off the cement floor, gazing into the dark space under the stairs, as if a blow was about to fall.

"Look what I have for you," I said, and held the chicken out to her, right under her nose, so she could catch a good whiff of it. I thought she would snatch it up greedily, but she didn't. She tried to ignore me, feigning disinterest, pushing herself further into the corner. She was becoming noticeably more worried and distressed. It's as if she wanted the treat so badly it scared her, and that made her all the more suspicious and upset. If she took the food, something seemed to be telling her, her fate would be sealed, and something terrible would befall her. The more she wanted it, the more fearful and nervous she became; she wanted to run, but there was nowhere to go. Her uneasiness translated to me, and I backed myself out of the cave.

"That's all right, girl," I tried to soothe her. "Here you go!" I said, and tossed one of the tasty morsels to her, inside the cave. She glanced fearfully aside and then, with all the courage and gusto she could muster, snatched up the treat, chewed it quickly and swallowed, then waited for the hammer to fall. But of course, it didn't.

"Good girl!" I congratulated her. (I would say these two words at least a zillion times in the next year; she needed constant encouragement and praise, and permission, to accomplish even the smallest task.) I tossed another piece to her, which she took a little easier, but still cautiously, then she waited again for the repercussions; but there were none. "Good girl!" I told her again. She started to relax a bit and waited passively for the next tidbit to fall into her lap. Daniel watched all of this from the armchair, that sat several feet back from the opening to her cave. "Go ahead in and see her," I suggested to him, "she'll let you pet her." But he declined. He was very mindful of the creature's comfort, and didn't want to be intrusive. "There'll be plenty of time," he said. She had not been out from under the stairs all day.

"We should try and get her to go outside," I suggested. I thought it would be good for her to see that there still was a world out there, and she probably needed to relieve herself. I got the long leash from the stairwell and hooked her up.

"Come on, Koko," I urged her, tugging at the leash. She plastered herself firmly against the back wall. "Let's go outside and take a walk," I cajoled her, but she wouldn't budge. I looked down at her, perplexed, careful not to make direct eye contact. (Whenever our eyes did accidentally meet, a violent and uncontrollable jolt would pervade her body and a pained expression would fill her face, as if she'd been struck; so I tried to avoid it.) I turned my back on her and tugged on the leash some more, but she remained stalwart. I tried tempting her out with a tasty bite of chicken, but that proved counterproductive, making her more suspicious and resolute: she wasn't going anywhere. This looked like a job for Bandit.

"Let's bring Bandit down," I suggested to Daniel. "She'll come out for him!" I could have dragged her from that place, but I really didn't think that would be helpful in the long run. She would come out on her own, sort of. Daniel went outside to get Bandit.

"Come on, Bandit," I said, calling up to him from the basement. He stood on the landing and stared blankly down at me. "Come on, boy!" I said, and motioned for him to come down. He started to turn away. "I've got a treat!" I said. That's all it took, and down the stairs he came. I led him over to the place underneath the stairs and pointed at Koko. "Look who's here!" I said, brightly. Bandit looked at Koko, then looked up at me, puzzled. What was this animal doing there, in the dark and dank, he wondered, and underneath the stairs, of all places? He wasn't impressed, and turned to go. I blocked his path; he barked in protest. Koko's ears perked up at the sound. She got up slowly and tentatively stepped out into the light, blinking her eyes. She seemed willing then, to follow Bandit. She trailed him up the stairs and out the back door. I followed behind her, holding onto the leash.

I led her around the yard, staying a safe distance away from the back fence. She walked with me obligingly, but her heart just wasn't in it. She wanted just to stand, but I prodded her on. When she stopped again I squatted down beside her. Slowly, so as not to frighten her, I placed my arm over her back and buried my fingers into the thick mane around her neck. Her hair was long and coarse. I gently massaged her chest. I told her how pretty she was, and how glad we were to have her with us. She leaned away from me slightly, unsure of whether to like this new sensation or not. The strangeness of it made her nervous, and I didn't press the matter. We traveled the perimeter of the yard one more time. Bandit watched from a distance. It was a balmy two-below and the wind had died down. Koko's eyes were lifeless and dull. She didn't seem terribly excited to be out, like I thought she would be. "Well, that's enough for now, huh girl?" I said. It had been a bewildering day. As soon as I opened the back door, she scurried down the stairs to plant herself back in the hollow cave. Clarrise called then, and said her and Norman were on the way.

"How are the cats?" was one of the first questions Clarrise asked, when they arrived. Oh yeah, I remembered, the cats. . . .

We had two black cats: Beanie and Cecil were their names. (Beanie was the one with the white spot on her chest.) They were brother and sister, littermates, about ten or eleven years old. Clarrise had voiced some concern (as had Daniel) about the cats, when we were first discussing the prospect of bringing Koko into the household. (Clarrise was as enamored with this species, as she was with the dogs.) I wasn't concerned about them. I knew if they made it through the first few seconds, they would be fine.

They were wise and wily creatures, the cats, and knew how to make themselves scarce. They never showed themselves when visitors came, shy and anti-social creatures that they were, and kept close tabs on the comings and goings around the house. The cats had their kitty-door in the basement, above and to the left of Koko's cave, and came and went as they pleased. An old wooden step-ladder rose to the shelf that led to the kitty-door, high above the floor. There was another high shelf on the other wall, where they liked to hang out. Besides, I goaded Clarrise, cats were expendable creatures, and black ones in particular were a dime a dozen; they could easily be replaced. I hadn't noticed any traces of black fur, or cat remains in Koko's cave, I said, so I assumed they were around somewhere. Clarrise squinted at me and shuddered at my callousness, unsure of whether I was serious or not. (But my lack of fondness for the animal was true; I could tolerate them in small doses, and respected them, as one of God's many creatures, but my affinity for them was negate. I just didn't understand them, their motives or thinking; they could be aloof and clingy, all at the same time, and I found it rather irritating.) But yes, we would have to think about the cats. We would move their act up to the second floor, their food and their litterbox, so they needn't even venture into the basement, for now. (They seldom went outside, during the winter, and wouldn't miss having access to the kitty-door.) It would be a long time before the cats came out.

"Shall we go down and see her?" I asked. The inevitable moment had arrived. Thus far, Norman hadn't spoken a word. We trooped down the basement to view the captive.

Koko was pressed back in her cave, much as she'd been before. We stayed back and looked at her. She was very uneasy. I told Norman it would be all right to pet her, she was very docile. He squatted down and approached her slowly, speaking in a soothing tone. He let her smell him, then stroked her gently with the back of his hand. I'm sure she recognized him as the guy from the river; she was very astute, and he had spent some time there.

We tried to coax her to come out with some tidbits of chicken. She stood up and took a step out. She wouldn't be hand-fed the meat, but would greedily gobble it up off the floor. The slightest untoward motion would send her scurrying back into her cave, to gaze out with watchful eyes; she was very skittish. Norman asked, gazing at the floor, if she'd been outside at all. I told him she had, but it had taken Bandit to convince her. Daniel and Clarrise chattered in the background. Koko looked at us looking at her; she was in obvious discomfort. I decided visiting hours were over and herded us back upstairs. Norman was off to rescue the clothes from the laundromat, down the street, and would pick Clarrise up on his way home from there. She stayed a while longer. She offered to make some signs, to post down at the river, to inform people that the stray had a new home and that she was safe and being well-cared for. There was sure to be some concern over her sudden disappearance. The animal had developed quite a following there, among the regular goers.

Clarrise had previously placed a sign at the river, the day we found the tire tracks in the snow, earlier in the week. She had printed, in black marker, on a large piece of cardboard, something to the effect that "alot of effort has been made to keep this animal alive during the frigid temperatures" and that "before any action is taken against her, please call . . . " and she left her phone number there, nailed to a tree. A bold move, indeed! I thought.

And it seemed only right, that people should know the animal was safe, but I emphasized that we were private people, and she shouldn't give away the animal's location or too much information. One thing Koko didn't need, was a parade of people coming by to stare at her through the fence, and that could happen. She needed peace and quiet, and to feel safe in her new home. For now, we would keep her under wraps.

Also, two camps had clearly developed. One camp believed that the animal should be left alone; that a wild creature should be left in the wild. And in almost any case, that would be true. But this was definitely not the wilderness. We were smack in the middle of the large, Twin Cities metropolitan area, with a view to the downtown. The other camp felt compassion for her, and wished that somebody could do something to save her. At any rate, it was the former's attitude that worried me. You never knew what lengths people would go to, to proffer their beliefs. Both Daniel and I stressed the fact, that we wanted to remain anonymous. Clarrise seemed to understand, and promised to be vague.

We closed up shop early that night; we were all exhausted. I went downstairs to say good-night to Koko, and to tuck a worn pair of sweatpants into the corner of her cave: I thought it might help her get accustomed to my scent. She was there, very much as we had left her.

Her eyes watched me benignly. She rolled onto her side and lifted her hind leg to me as before. I eased myself down in the door of her cave and leaned against the hard, concrete wall. The cement floor was very cold. I reached over and up between her front legs, to scratch her chest. With my other hand, I exerted a light pressure on her rear haunch, easing her leg to close. "It doesn't have to be like that, girl," I told her. "Here's where it's at," I said, scratching her chest more vigorously, "all up front with us."

She sat prone then, and clutched my forearm between her front legs. Holding my hand in her paws, she began to very slowly, very deliberately, lick the tips of my fingers. Her big, brown eyes watched me carefully. Something profound passed between us then. Perhaps it was just that my skin was so cold, but her tongue felt piercingly hot. And so were my eyes, hot with tears. She touched me someplace deep inside, where no one ever goes.

I left her then, and departed, headed back up to the topside world, a little in a daze, feeling as though I'd been kissed by an angel, feeling like the anointed one.

XX.
The Appointment

The first night passed peacefully. Bandit started out on the bed as usual, to have his ears "attended to," but soon took his place on the floor, at its foot. (Our bed was simply a queen-size mattress, laid on the floor. We had just never gotten around to getting the box springs and frame, and with Bandit's advancing age, it was all he could do sometimes, just to get up on this.) We left the door to the basement open, giving Koko access to the house. I was afraid that she might wake up during the night, feeling strange and alone, and I didn't want her to feel like she'd been abandoned again. I was sure, if there was any commotion, I would be aroused. But my sleep was so sound, I doubt I would have heard her, had she ripped the place apart. I awoke the next morning with all the anticipation of a child on Christmas morning.

I like to get up early, to sit in the heavy silence of a fresh, new day. To rise before the rest of the world arose; to get a jump on the day. To sit and compose myself, and make a mental list of things I should do, things I had to do, and things I wanted to do, putting off until tomorrow, whatever I could. And having that done, I could sit back and relax, and sip my coffee, and settle into the peace and tranquillity of the day-not-yet-born. But ready I would be, and waiting, patiently for the dawn.

Koko came up to the back door landing as I prepared the morning's first pot of coffee. As soon as she saw that I saw her, she turned and ran back down the stairs. She probably needs to go out, I thought. Bandit was already at the back door, waiting. I let him out. Koko looked up at me from the basement, all wide-eyed (she already had a firm hold on my heartstrings). "Do you want to go out too?" I asked her. I threw on my coat and boots and took the leash from the hook. She ran back to huddle in her cave. I followed her there and hooked her up to the leash. (When she was in her cave, you could approach her and hook her up; otherwise, she was totally elusive. And she knew I would come for her there, but still, that's where she always fled.) With a little coaxing, she came along and we went outside.

She went to the triangle, where Bandit had already posted himself, and nudged him a couple of times with her muzzle. He raised his head and watched as Koko and I investigated the boundaries of the yard. The mercury had risen during the night and it was already in the 'teens. The weather had finally broke. The sky was clear; it promised to be a great day, and we deserved it. When I determined the coffee was ready we headed back inside (I didn't dare leave her in the yard unattended). Koko immediately went back to her cave.

I watched the morning news and drank my coffee, planning to call the veterinary clinic when it opened, at eight. I wanted to see about getting Koko checked for worms. Clarrise seemed to think she had them; I thought her symptoms might also be attributed to a poor diet. But we could easily find out, and it wouldn't require that I bring her in. Soon, Daniel was up.

As soon as the time was right, I placed the call to Dr. Goodman's office. We were fortunate to have him as our vet. We had been referred to him by some nutty lady we met at the lake one day. He was a very kind and compassionate man, and had seen us through the ordeal of the summer before, when Bandit was deathly ill. He took my concerns seriously and never made me feel like an overwrought pet-owner, encouraging me to call anytime I had a question, or if things didn't look just right; he even examined Bandit for free one time, when he was on the road to his recovery, but seemed to me, to be in relapse. He was very understanding. He had saved Bandit's life.

I spoke to the lady at the desk. She, on the other hand, made me nervous. I refer to her affectionately as the "vet-tech lady," although I'm unsure of her actual position (I have never been one to pry). She is a tall, spectacled, angular-faced woman who, no matter how prepared I was, always caught me off guard, asking me questions, offering suggestions, had I tried or done, this or that, before granting me an audience with the good doctor. Grilling me, in effect. (But I do understand her motives: otherwise, the man might be on the phone all day, answering inane questions, and allaying the fears of neurotic pet-owners.) Still, I was always wary of her, and of receiving from her, the librarian-look: the look you got from the librarian when some loose remark, said too loudly, got the rest of the class snickering. But most of my calls were just routine, setting up appointments for shots, or to pick up some minor remedy. Then I would take a big gulp of air, and try not to stutter and stammer, as I told her what I needed.

I explained to her how we had acquired this stray animal, and that I was afraid she might have worms. She advised me to bring in a stool sample, at my earliest convenience. I told her I hadn't been able to round one up yet, but should be able to, by Monday. Then she advised me to bring her in as soon as possible for shots. She was pretty emphatic about it. I hadn't even thought of it, but I knew she was right. I didn't know how I could possibly do it though, I whined and begged her, for the animal was hopelessly untamed; I tried to explain.

"Just put her on a choke-chain (so she can't get away from you), and bring her in," she explained patiently, and as usual, I felt like a simpleton. As I looked around for my dunce-cap, a vision of the scared and cowering, terrified-of-people, and not-to-keen-on-cars Koko dashed through my mind. It was not a pretty picture. "Use a muzzle, if you have to," she said very matter-of-factly, "just bring her in. . . ." And I did see the logic in her approach. After all, it was only a dog, weighing no more than fifty pounds or so, so what was the problem? I would just bring her in! I made the appointment for Monday morning. It was Friday. That would give me time to prepare, and hopefully by then, I would have the necessary sample. I tried not to dwell on it over the weekend.

By then, Bandit was chomping at the bit and ready for his morning outing. Koko came up to see what the fuss was all about, hearing Bandit's frantic and pleading barking. (Bandit didn't just get excited, like a normal dog at walk-time, he went berserk: it was as if he'd never been on a walk before, and if we didn't go right this very *minute*, we would probably never get to go at all!) As soon as any advance was made in her direction, Koko would high-tail it back through the kitchen. Daniel offered to take Bandit, thinking Koko might be more at ease, left in my company. They took off out the front door.

We were normally back door people, but had decided for now, to abandon that, hoping Koko would think the only legitimate way out was through the front; then maybe she wouldn't focus so much attention on the back fence and gate. For now, there was no back gate (it was pretty much boarded up anyway). And eventually, there would be no more garage. Koko showed a tendency to want to follow the car, so we began to park it out on the street, when we knew we would be needing it.

In all the excitement of getting Bandit underway, Koko had fled to her cave. I went down to keep her company. She still hadn't eaten a thing, or touched the water in the bowl. I wondered, maybe water-in-a-bowl was just too much for her to comprehend? I had often seen her gulping down snow at the river. I found a deep dishpan and filled it with fresh, unspoiled snow from the side of the house. I brought it down to the basement and set it on the floor. That, she could relate to. When Bandit came back, we used him again to persuade her outside.

We walked around the backyard for awhile. The temperature was near twenty and the sun was shining bright. For the first time, I took a good look at her in the light of day and tried to discern her age. Because of her size, and the size of her teeth, I thought she must be at least a year old. But knowing that most puppies are born in the spring or early summer, that would make her a year-and-a-half, almost two years old, and that just didn't seem right. If she *was* that old, where had she spent the previous time? And how had she ended up so wild? Had she simply fallen from the sky, that fateful Christmas Eve, to land at that place on the hill, where we found her? It just didn't fit. And as she stood there in the snow, I noticed that her front claws failed to even touch the ground, as if she was sitting back on her heels, and I chalked that up to immaturity. But it was her constant willingness to play, and her persistent need to chew on everything, and explore, that would finally convince us, she was nothing more than a puppy—a big puppy. And her tendency to grow.

She grew in spurts and all out of proportion. First her hind legs would grow, leaving the front ones behind. Then her paws would grow too large and clumsy. Then her head would get big, and look too huge for her long and slender body. But that would eventually catch up, and within a year-and-a-half, everything would even out, and fill out, until she became the splendid perfection she is today, more than doubling Bandit in weight and size. We started to call her Baby Huey as she grew, and grew, out of every harness and collar we had. But for now, she was only a worn and defeated puppy, robbed of her youth. How had she ever managed alone, being so young and all? I wondered. Then I let her return to her cave, where she seemed to feel the safest, and where she slept most of the day away.

Clarrise stopped by briefly that afternoon, to see how we were managing. She had a lot of ideas, and input from different people she had spoken to, with advice on how best to manage this feral creature. I listened politely, but I knew, I was pretty much on my own in this. Only Koko could dictate what needed to be done, and I would take my cues from her. Somehow, some way, I would reach her; if only out of sheer determination. I had no idea where the journey would take me, or just how long and hard it would be.

XXI.
Hellhound

Things were going rather well, I thought. Actually, it was going much better than I had expected it would. Koko was silent and unobtrusive: you would hardly know she was there, planted away, underneath the stairs (though her presence filled the house). I took her out regularly on the leash, to walk her around the yard, but she seemed most content just to stay hidden away. We had another peaceful night. The next day was Saturday and the mercury climbed into the upper twenties. Koko's eyes would light a little, whenever Bandit was near, but otherwise she remained aloof, her eyes staring off to someplace, far away. She still had shown no interest in food or drink. I tried to entice her to play the rope-game, but she was easily distracted by any movement or sound.

Koko was an animal on the run. Her chief motivating instinct was also the most basic one: survival. And everything and everybody seemed to threaten that. Her immediate response was to escape: to run, to hide, to evade, to elude. Somehow, I had to convince her that it was time to stop running. I had to prove to her that this was her space, her home, and she was safe here. I would be her guardian and protector, her mentor in this new world. She would see that there was life outside these walls, but she would have to learn to deal with it all on different terms. Like it or not, in a civilized society, there were rules to be followed. There would be fences and collars and leashes. There would be traffic and houses and people everywhere, popping out unexpectedly from alleyways and doorways and cars that were parked along the curb. And that was her biggest fear: people. She could stand the loud city buses, that spewed exhaust in her face, the dogs that barked from their yards as we passed, the cars that rolled by with clanking and noisy mufflers, all of these things only bothered her slightly. But it was the appearance of a human form, no matter how near or far, that once she caught sight of (and she was always looking), would set her into a spin, and off in sheer panic. And that is the way it always would be (though as the years passed, to a lesser degree).

I thought it might be therapeutic for her to accompany us on Bandit's evening walk. She could see for herself that the world outside did still exist, but she would visit it on these new terms. I would put one of Bandit's old harnesses on her, with one leash attached, and the nylon choke-collar, with another leash attached to that. There was no way she was getting away from me, I thought. And with Bandit and Daniel in the lead, we headed out the front door. She was scared and apprehensive to go, but with Bandit as the bait, she soon followed along. It was dark and quiet out. We headed out into the neighborhood streets, deliberately not toward the river.

Koko walked obediently beside me. She walked in a crouching fashion with her tail tucked down and between her legs. Her eyes and nose scouted nervously as we walked. She started at even the slightest sound and watched with anxiety, the lit windows of the houses as we passed, waiting for the two-legged ogres to appear. But the walk was uneventful. We made it down the block and around the next. Bandit took care of his business and we headed home. Koko was stressed out and had obviously had enough. It was upon our return, from her first time out in the world in three days, that we met Koko's evil twin, Koko-Loco.

Once out, Koko could not be contained. When we returned, she was no longer content just to retire to her cave, to be the silent and forlorn creature she was before. Her eyes were filled with a new fire, as she realized that the world was out there waiting, just as she had left it. She yearned to be free, *burned* to be free, to relive and regain her wildness again. But it could never again be that way, and it would tear me apart, to keep her from it.

Once back inside, Koko raced brazenly through the house, from back door to front, and back to front again. She concentrated her attentions mostly on the front, for that is the way by which we had left. Her nose was drawn to the windows and door, anywhere that a cold blast of fresh air came in, and in this drafty old house, that was places o' plenty. She could smell freedom, but she couldn't get to it. She took the floor-length drapes, in the front room, in her teeth and began to pull, hoping to tender her goal. It didn't take much to dissuade her from that, but the force of her desire and the power inherent in her was an unnerving thing to behold. Afraid of the damage she could bestow, I quickly got her in control and reattached her to the leash. She thrashed against it and pulled me to the front door, begging to have it laid open. But of course, it couldn't be done.

I persuaded her back down the stairs, to the basement, and led her to her cave, but she wanted none of it. She saw me now only as an obstacle to her freedom, and pushed boldly by me and crawled freely over me as I tried to block her exit to the stairs. She exhibited not a snarl, or tendency to bite, but passively and forceably, made her intentions known: she wanted out. That casual stroll around the block had unleashed the beast within, and rekindled a fire that burned fierce and deep. The situation was rapidly getting out-of-control and a fear rose within me; I was afraid for her, and afraid for me. She was a force to be reckoned with, and it took all of my persuasive powers to hold her there. I was at a loss: what to do next? Then the solution came clear. "I forgot to call Clarrise!" I said, and handed the leash to the astonished Daniel. I fled up the stairs before he could protest.

It was almost nine-thirty. I had told Clarrise I would call her if there were any new developments, and this seemed to qualify as one. The beast was out! It was the reaction we had expected from the beginning, but we had been lulled into a sense of complacency, by her collapsed behavior; I was not at all prepared for this, now.

"She's come undone!" was basically what I told Clarrise. "She's gone wild!" I said, and she *must* have noticed the slight tremble and bit of panic in my voice. She conferred with Norman. He conveyed, through Clarrise, that it was probably a good sign: she had lapsed out of her comatose state and was ready to live again. Something about what he said rang true, but being in the heat of it, I was hard to convince.

As I talked on the phone, Daniel sat in the basement with Koko on the leash, trying to soothe her and calm her down. She wouldn't be consoled. She came up to him and got right in his face. She stood momentarily, with her muzzle only inches from his face, and with a deep and wild look in her eyes (that had him praying for redemption), she leaned forward and, with a large swipe from her tongue, planted a kiss squarely on his bare forehead. Then she was back at it, straining at the leash, trying to get free. It was as if she wanted to apologize for her behavior, but she couldn't help herself. She was persistent and untiring. I hung up from Clarrise, having gained no suggestions, and went to relieve Daniel.

I tried again, to get her comfortable in her cave, but that wasn't what she had in mind. I decided to take her back outside and pace her around for awhile, hoping she would calm down and relax. But things were no better out there. She was desperate to get free. The night was calling her. She paced frantically back and forth, concentrating her efforts on the back section, where she had almost escaped before. I could see that she was gathering herself to spring. I tugged gently on the leash and told her "no!"; I steered her toward the center of the yard. Thankfully, it was still near twenty degrees, and the weather wasn't a factor.

Suddenly, Koko was up on her hind legs, against me. Her front paws clawed frantically at my chest and shoulders. I felt a slight panic rise within me. What was she doing? Her eyes pleaded with me and begged me to release her. "Koko," I said, "I just can't do it!" My heart was breaking, and it pounded in my throat. She pawed at me furiously. Her back feet left the ground as she leapt at me excitedly. She knew that I was the way out, but she didn't know how. It was as if she thought she could climb up me, and by that way somehow, make her escape. Daniel appeared at the back door as the drama played out, and peered at us through the darkness. He watched nervously.

"Better be careful of her, " he advised. He was a little afraid of what she might do, and that I might accidentally get hurt. But she never hurt me, though she did leave some awesome claw marks in the soft leather of my jacket, which when I look at today, always takes me back to that wild, moonlit night. "You better come in, now, " Daniel advised, "it's getting close to midnight."

I led Koko back in and straight down the stairs. I knew she was not ready to sleep; she was wound tight. But I sure was, and I knew Daniel and Bandit were too. We decided to just shut her in the basement, hoping eventually, she would wear herself out. But it was impossible to sleep, as things in the basement crashed and banged. I thought I'd better go and see.

Koko had climbed the scrap-wood pile against the north wall, and was clawing frantically against the concrete wall, trying to climb her way to the one window there. She darted off as soon as I approached and we played hide-and-seek around the furnace. Finally, I was able to constrain her. I put her on the leash and led her to the cave. I pushed her in and posted myself in the doorway, blocking her exit. But she would not be confined. She crawled up to the smallest space, under the stairs, and through the bottom shelf of the workbench, then headed back up the stairs. She was relentless. She pawed and clawed at the back door frantically. She jumped up to the door's high window, and pulled at the plastic mini-blinds that hung there, leaving her teeth marks in them. She was drawn by the stars and the cold night air. I grabbed the leash and dragged her back down the stairs and shoved her in her cave again. This time I held tight to the leash.

"No, Koko," I tried to calm her. "You've just got to settle down now." I stroked her cheek and neck. She lay in her cave panting. Her eyes were wild and panicked. Soon, Daniel's voice came calling down the stairs.

"Are you okay?" he asked. I told him I was fine, but that if anybody was going to get any sleep tonight, I would probably have to stay with her awhile. He told me to be careful and I said I would.

I sat in the door to her cave, holding onto the leash. I was exhausted, and she seemed so too. But after a brief respite, she was up and at it again. She bullied right by me and headed for the stairs. I prevented her progress. We paced around the basement, but she was insistent, and there was no recourse but to take her back outside. We paced around the yard. Then we went in again. I tried to hold her to her cave, but she was tough; I was weary. I woke up the next morning, rolled up in a sleeping bag on the concrete floor, the leash still dangling from my hand, Koko fast asleep on the other end.

I went upstairs in the silent hour: the darkest one, before the dawn. The house was quiet. Daniel was sound asleep in bed. Bandit was in the living room and stirred and stretched as I made the coffee. It was just after six. He went out to post himself in the straw of his triangle, where he would wait for his time to go. I sipped my coffee in the dark morning, listening to the Weather Channel, perusing the tv guide for something to view. The forecaster spoke of a glowing day, sunny and warm; what a relief to hear! It was all I needed to raise my tired spirits. Then I noticed that the "Adventures of Johnny Quest" was coming on, at half-past. I hadn't seen that show in years, and it was a kick to see the little, white cartoon dog with the black mask, that Bandit had been named after, cavorting across the screen again! He reminded me so much of my own Bandit, in his younger years, and I laughed at him out loud. It made me feel years younger, and took me back to that time. I sat in the fleeting peace and calm of the brand new day, wondering what it had in store.

XXII.
The Return of Hellhound

As usual, Bandit raised the roof at walk-time, rousting Koko from her deflated slumber, to come and see what the fuss was all about. We hurried out the front door, leaving Daniel and her behind. It was good to be out. It was a nice morning, with the temperature reaching toward twenty degrees. I let Bandit lead me astray and he was in his glory; we took longer than usual. When we returned it was Koko's turn and I took her out into the backyard on a leash.

The good twin had returned during the night and Koko was back to her meek and mild self. We criss-crossed the yard, poked around in the snow a little, and played the rope-game with just a little more vigor. She seemed mildly more content and interested in her surroundings. She still had on Bandit's old harness, from the raucous night before. I hooked a twelve foot leash to it, and let her loose, to explore the yard on her own terms. After years of practice with Bandit, I was pretty sure I could dive for the leash and grab a hold of it fast enough to foil any escape attempt, if she got it into her head to jump. I shadowed her though, and hovered between her and the back fence where she seemed the most prone to try. She tried unsuccessfully to provoke Bandit, and unenthusiastically, pounced on a dead leaf, but her mind was on escape, and she was ever watchful for the slightest breech in security to affect it. She knew she was loose, but she knew I was watching her every move too. Let the game begin! It was her move, and she was in check.

Two crows sat squawking from the power pole by the corner. Koko watched them with interest. I wondered if they were her friends from the river, come by to say hello. It was impossible to know for sure, because all crows look pretty much alike, but something told me, they were. And almost every morning thereafter, two crows would come by, as if on their morning rounds, to sit in the trees or on the power lines, or to Caw! at each other from distant treetops. Dried crusts of bread and old, worn-out bones started to appear in the yard. Had they been dropped there deliberately, or by default? Who can say; I only know what I know.

I was getting increasingly nervous, with Koko untendered and roaming the yard. I could sense the energy in her building the longer she remained unrestrained. As she stood stone-still, watching a squirrel make its way down the tree, I edged up to her and picked up the end of the leash. She immediately knew she was "caught," you could just see it in her eyes. She slunk away from me and hid behind the tree.

The huge maple that sat in the front-quarter of the backyard was a favorite place of the squirrels and blue jays. Its mammoth trunk divided into a triad of trunks, each a considerable circumference by itself, which reached toward the sky. A large crotch formed in the tree where the triumvirate met, about five feet off the ground. It was a perfect place to put peanuts and sunflower seeds for our wintertime guests. It was good viewing from the kitchen window, as the squirrels and jays competed for the nuts, chasing and confronting each other, running in circles, up and down and around the tree. When the squirrel was ready to leave, it would climb to one of the highest branches, balance delicately at its very end, and make the precarious leap to the reaching boughs of the pine. Then it would scurry down that trunk and up and over the roof of the garage, never having to step foot in the yard. But Bandit's interest in squirrel-chasing was on the wane, and the squirrels had become bold and lax. But there was a new kid in town, and I had a feeling that Koko would take up where he left off. One day soon, that overconfident squirrel would get the surprise of its lifetime.

After the morning out, Koko slept the day away in her cave. We had been up most of the night before. I took advantage of the time and got some sleep myself. (When she was up and about, I was up; when she slept, I slept. It would be that way for weeks to come.) I brought Bandit in to give him some added attention. But Bandit didn't seem to mind all the attention I was paying to Koko: he was secure in his position. As long as it didn't interfere with his walks, what I did on my own time was my business. If I wanted to spend it on this strange creature, that was all right with him. But I was alert for any sign of jealousy or sense of displacement in him, and was careful to let him know that he was still, and always would be, my Number One.

He actually might have received more attention after Koko's arrival than before she came, owing to the amount of time I spent outdoors, especially in the winter. Previously, I seldom ventured out in the winter voluntarily, as a chill would set into my bones in late September, and stay until the Fourth of July. Bandit was always outside. I preferred to stay in, with the curtains drawn against the cold, to seek my refuge there and escape into words and music, and far too much television. All of that changed with Koko's coming. I learned to live in and survive the cold; maybe not to appreciate winter's severe bite, but to respect it, and the season's unique flavor. I would never say I looked forward to its coming, but I knew its coming was inevitable and steeled myself for its onslaught. And it wasn't winter's coming that I minded, but its staying, on and on and on, sometimes into late April and even early May. But the dogs loved it. They seemed to feel most at home, nestled in a heaping bed of straw, with the cold wind and snow in their faces. But today was a welcome reprieve from all that.

By late afternoon the temperature had passed the freezing mark; the January thaw was in full swing. I decided to take Bandit back to Thirty-sixth Street for our afternoon walk, to revisit the scene of the crime. He loved to go there, and we hadn't been to the river for days.

It felt strange and very quiet as we approached the hill. Although the weather was fine and it was a Sunday, there was not a soul in sight. Clarrise had posted the signs, just as she had said she would, on several trees along the trail. They read, "Change of Address! Notice to all of you who cared for the lost pup from Christmas Eve on, making her life possible in the freezing temperatures. She has moved on to a new family and home, and in time will be back to visit. Thank you!" (I still have one of the signs in my file, a keepsake from those days gone by.) The message was succinct, and very vague, just as we had asked, and I was relieved.

I thought of all the people who had made it their business to care for her, and were now left to wonder; and I hoped we *could* someday come back for a visit. But for now, I thought it would be best to keep Koko far away from the river, and her untamed past. (I had no idea at the time, just how far-gone she really was. The fearful behavior she exhibited was just a manifestation of her basic and overall wildness.) The pile of straw and the bales were gone. Only straw-dust and the dull scratchings of a rake in the snow remained, tell-tale signs of what had taken place here. (Clarrise and Norman had, very conscientiously, cleaned up the area.) I left the hill that day with an acute sense of something lost, something that could never be regained. But buried in that, a sense of wonderment at what had begun. It would be some time, before I returned to that place on the hill again.

Koko finally began to eat. She was very nervous and flighty, when food was offered, as if it would lead to her final undoing. I suspect she was tempted many times, to surrender herself for a morsel of food. And it probably worked, once. She was much too cagey for that now. I would set down the dinner bowls, and walk away. Only then would she approach to feed. And if Bandit didn't eat his, which was often the case, she would gobble his down too; he was glad to be rid of it. (He would get a special dinner, later.) She would eat until she threw up. But she still wouldn't take water from a bowl. Rather, she would jab at it with her front foot, until she had successfully tipped the bowl over and spilled its contents onto the ground. Then she would sip it up from there.

We decided not to take Koko out that evening, hoping to avoid the antics of the night before, and the return of hellhound. She had slept quietly through the day, and we were hoping for a peaceful night: but it was not to be. As the sun began to set and night rolled in, Koko grew increasingly more restless and agitated. It was her time, and she could not be consoled. I walked her endlessly around the yard, but it wasn't what she wanted. Her eyes looked wild and were full of that fire. I tried to confine her to the basement, but she struggled away and up the stairs, to claw frantically, though futilely, at the back door. (Where to this day, the deep grooves in the wood from her claws still remain, a testament to the wildness that she was.) She wouldn't be kept away from the window in the back door: she could smell the fresh air and sense the outdoors that lay just beyond. It was near midnight again, and she was totally sprung.

I left Koko in the basement and went to check on Daniel and Bandit, who were lying on the bed. I was hoping for some suggestions. They both rolled their eyes and looked at me, accusingly. I got the message. "I'm going to get her settled down," I promised, "she will settle down." I headed out of there and back for the basement.

"What have we done?" Daniel cried out behind me, moaning, "maybe we've made a mistake!" But I knew it was too late for questions like that. I couldn't believe he was wiener-ing out on me already. I knew then that I was on my own, and although tired and weary myself, there was nothing else to do but carry on.

"She'll be okay," I assured him, and somehow in my heart, I knew she would be. If we could just make it from here to there, without sinking the whole ship and losing the crew; I sensed a mutiny.

I rounded up Koko and brought her back downstairs. I tried to keep her in her cave, or at least, keep her quiet. But she was adamant, and escaped by me again, to focus her attention on the back door. She galloped up and down the basement stairs, from the window to the door and back to the window. She could smell the night, she could see the night, and she tried desperately to reach it. She played peek-a-boo around the furnace and would not be caught. Finally, Daniel was up and at the top of the stairs, scolding us both, as if either one of us had any control.

"We're going to have to put some plywood up over these windows, or she'll never leave them alone!" I shouted back. So we got to work, in the middle of the night, cutting up plywood and screwing it over the windows, shutting out the night for good. It worked, to some extent. She forgot about the window and concentrated her efforts solely on clawing her way through the back door. I needed a break, and left her there, shut in the basement.

My body felt strained but my eyes were wide awake. Koko was relentless on the other side of the bedroom wall, working away at the back door. Then she would claw to be let in the house. The broom closet that was there, had become the recycling room, and she tore through the paper bags full of empty Coke cans and plastic milk jugs with abandon, kicking and throwing them all asunder. She was in a real tantrum. Sleep was impossible and Daniel was at his wit's end. He and Bandit glowered at me. "I guess I'll just have to take her outside again," I said.

"Well you can't stay out there with her all night!" Daniel reproached me, as if it was my choice to do that. I didn't think it was fair, that he be taking it out on me. What did he expect me to do then? I wondered. But he had no suggestions. Just do something. I could fight with him, or I could fight with Koko. I got up and headed for the basement.

I grabbed the leash and headed down the stairs after Koko. It was close to one-thirty in the morning. We went outside and stood in the yard. In the distance, a dog barked. Other than that, the city night was silent. We stood under the stars and looked at the moon. It would soon be full. Then Koko was on me again, up on her hind legs, imploring me to set her free. I felt torn. I felt so sorry for her: she didn't understand why it just couldn't be. And then I thought, was it really worth it, and who was I, to take this from her? She wanted it so badly, and for just a moment, I almost gave in. I was tempted to fling open the gate and set her free. To let her return to the world she so desired. But reason gained voice, and I knew, she would never survive.

"Oh, Koko," I begged her, while the tears filled my eyes, "just give me a chance. You'll see, there is a place for you here. Just give it a chance." Eventually, we returned to the confines of the concrete prison below. I slept beside her again, on the floor, as exhaustion swept in, and sleep finally came. We had to be at the veterinary clinic, first thing in the morning.

XXIII.
"Blondie"

The trip to the doctor's office on Monday morning was every bit as tragic and traumatic as I had imagined it would be. Koko was immediately suspicious, sensing something was afoot. (She probably picked up on my own nervousness.) Even with the harness, choke-collar, and two leashes on, Koko refused to be budged from under the tree. She looked nervously over to Bandit, who watched the scene with puzzled interest. We had backed the car out of the garage, onto the cement slab, and Bandit took that into consideration, wondering if we were *all* going for a ride? But he wasn't invited, and I think Koko realized that, and resisted even more. I tried pulling her with force to the back gate; she gagged on the choke-collar. I let up on that and started pulling her by her harness. We were making some progress, but sideways. As soon as she understood my intention, of bringing her to the car, she fell to her side and lay there, staring woefully up at me, with her legs folded tightly to her belly. I was getting exasperated. It was getting late.

"Oh, Koko," I tried to console her. "This is going to be every bit as bad as you think, and maybe even worse," I told her in a sing-song voice, knowing that she couldn't understand a word of what I was saying, but hoping my tone would encourage her.

"Don't tell her that!" Daniel admonished me, as if she could understand. I glared at him.

"Well," I said, looking down at the pathetic beast that lay on the ground before me, "better get Bandit." I sighed. I really hated to do it, but there was no other way. She looked up at me with hurt and fearful eyes.

Daniel called Bandit to the back gate. I *am* invited! he thought, and came bounding toward the gate and jumped into the backseat of the car. He stood there eagerly, waiting, his eyes shining with glee. I groaned. Koko was inspired though, and got up and walked tentatively nearer to the car. At the deciding moment, before she could flee, I straddled her back and picked up her front legs and duck-walked her to the car. I tried to hurl her into the backseat, but as soon as she realized my intention, she braced her front feet on the outside of the vehicle, and refused to be put in. I grabbed her front legs and aimed them in, behind the folded front-seat. (It was only a two-door vehicle, and for the first time, I saw the advantage of having a four-door.) I almost fell in on top of her, but she was in. Bandit barked excitedly in the back seat the whole time, anxious to be on his way. The sound resonated and bounced around inside the car until I thought my head would pop. Now we had to get him out. I held firmly onto Koko while Daniel escorted Bandit, who by now was totally perplexed, out the other door and back into the yard. He stood and watched through the slats in the gate as we pulled away, a hurt and confused look on his face. I felt a sharp pang of guilt, but promised myself that I would make it up to him when we got back.

The ride to the vet took no more than ten or fifteen agonizing minutes. Koko was terrified; she trembled uncontrollably the whole way. She was sure that every person on the road was out to get her, and would dive to the floor whenever a car pulled up beside us at a red light, and the driver happened to look over and notice her. Her eyes were wild with panic and her breath came hot and fast. We finally reached the clinic. I scooted her out of the car and up the few steps through the big, glass door. Before she knew to resist, we were in. She huddled on the mat in the waiting room, positive that the end was near. As soon as the stern-looking lady stepped out from the back and approached the counter, Koko lost it altogether. Though we had not been able to acquire one earlier, a "sample" now lay spread all over the waiting room floor. Koko swam through it and socked herself into the farthest corner, behind a large, potted plant. She looked frightened and humiliated. I looked at the lady, helplessly.

She acted nonchalant as Daniel reached for some paper towels to clean up the mess. She assured me that this was not the first time a dog had had an "accident" on the floor, and tried to relieve the situation by removing herself to the back. Soon, Dr. Goodman came out.

He was very mindful of the creature's comfort and stood at a distance, speaking in a soft and soothing tone. (I don't know what Koko thought, but it made me feel better.) He approached her slowly and knelt down beside her; he stroked her coat gently. She showed no reaction. Rather than drag her into the examining room, he administered the necessary shots and tests, right there in the corner, on the floor of the waiting room. And it was confirmed, she did have worms. I was a little embarrassed for Koko and myself, at the mess on the floor, but I had tried to warn them. (Though thereafter, before I brought Koko in for her yearly visits, the vet-tech lady would always remind me, not to feed her prior to bringing her in, to avoid a repeat of that performance.)

Koko seemed willing to stay plastered in the corner. I explained to the vet-tech lady, how she became so wild and out-of-control at night, and asked if they could prescribe a mild sedative for her. But she was unwilling, and said, that would only delay the inevitable process we had to go through. Then could you prescribe something for me? I asked facetiously, and laughed nervously. She gave me the librarian-look. She suggested that, like a new baby, Koko needed to have her schedule rearranged. If we could keep her up and active during the day, she would sleep better at night. It made sense. Dr. Goodman suggested using food, to quell and befriend her. And with any other animal, that was sound advice, but when it came to Koko, I knew that the introduction of food into an already tense situation only made it worse. He told me about two of his patients, a large male, and a full-grown female wolf that he treated, and how one time, the male had charged him. He never actually said he thought Koko *was* a wolf, but as he explained why he would not recommend them as pets, he added, "but the way you came upon *her* . . . " and left the sentence to dangle. But my head was spinning and I just wanted to get out of there. Koko was as unwilling to leave as she had been to enter, and I had to drag her from the corner and out the door. They both wished us good-luck as we left.

Daniel did a thorough and uncomplaining job of cleaning up the car when we got home. The feces spread all over Koko's extremities had transferred to the backseat. I took her directly to the basement and sponged her off. She stood passively and defeated. We had violated and invaded her horribly. I wasn't afraid that the experience had destroyed her trust in me, for there was none to destroy; I just wondered how far-reaching the effects would be, as I tried to establish a bond. She had not trusted me before, but neither had I given her any reason to distrust me. Now she looked at me evermore suspiciously and warily. I sat with her in the cave and tried to apologize, for causing such anguish. I left her to sleep it off.

Clarrise called to see how the trip to the doctor had gone. I told her the tragic and comedic high and low points of the visit. She listened, and chortled at Koko's dramatic reaction to the event, finding some amusement in the creature's discomfort; I failed to see the humor. I told her how they had suggested rearranging Koko's schedule, to keep her up during the day, so she would rest at night, but admitted I was not sure how to accomplish that feat. But Clarrise was fast with a solution. Her dogs were way beyond the play-stage, but she knew a spicy little cocker spaniel that might fit the bill. Koko loved to play with other dogs, and it sounded like a good idea. She was inhibited in her play with me, as I was of the human persuasion, and really needed to cut loose. Clarrise promised to come by after the dinner hour, with Blondie.

I let Koko sleep for awhile, to recover from the traumatic events of the morning, and to give her coat a chance to dry, from the sponge-bath I had given her earlier. But I was bound and determined to get some sleep tonight, and wasn't about to let her stay in seclusion too long. And it was a bright, sunny day out. The January thaw was well under way, with the temperature climbing toward thirty. I went downstairs to roust Koko and drag her up into the light of day. She tried to ignore me.

"Oh-no you don't," I told her, "we're going outside!" She looked up at me with sleepy eyes, as I tugged on the leash, trying to extricate her. She wished me to disappear. Finally, reluctantly, she came along, wondering I suppose, what evil thing I was going to do to her this time. "We're just going outside," I reassured her. "Look! There's Bandit!" I told her excitedly, as we exited the house. She went to him, head down, tail wagging ever so slightly. She poked at him with her nose and nuzzled his fur. He grumped and growled at being disturbed, but she was unaffected. I walked her to the pile of straw we had set up for her and knelt beside her. I stroked her gently and ran my fingers through her thick fur. Her coloring was unique and incredible.

She was every shade of gray, between black and white; but the only true white, was the kerchief-sized bib she wore on her throat, and the only true black was at the tip of her tail (as if it had been dipped in an ink-pot), and the softness under her chin (which would turn salt-and-pepper as she matured). The array of grays intermingled, to form complex patterns and markings, perfectly symmetrical on either side. Each hair was not one color, but many different shades, starting white next to her skin, and fading to black at the tip. The markings on her face would change and flow, chameleon-like, as she shed and gained her winter coat. She was extraordinary.

Koko's fear was tempered by an insatiable curiosity. Even though something worried her, she couldn't help but check it out. She was hyper-alert and totally aware of her surroundings. There would be no sneaking up on this girl! She judged each new sensation as to what effect it might have on her survival, and then reacted accordingly. Most everything, she saw as a threat. She was cautious and flighty. She seemed slightly more content to be in the yard, and did not try to surmount the fence, but decided on another tactic. She grabbed the corner of the waferboard in her teeth, and pulled on the corner of it, trying to release it from its anchor. She broke off a good chunk. She gnawed on the pickets of the gate, trying to open a hole there. Thankfully, the ground was hard and frozen, and she couldn't dig her way out. I guided her away from her task. I was hoping for a sign: if she would just once, lie down in the straw bed we had provided, I thought, she would be home. But it was all still too foreign, and she just couldn't relax. I was ready to go in, and she had to come in too. I allowed her to return to her cave, knowing Blondie would be by later to put the finishing touch on my plan to get a restful night. Not long after dinner, Clarrise came by with Blondie; and she was a spitfire.

Blondie was in the house and up on the table and on the couch and in the bedroom and down to the basement and back up, before we even made it through to the kitchen. Koko stood anxiously at the back door, aware of an alien canine force in the house. Bandit was unaware, until Blondie came flying out the back door. Daniel had Koko on the leash. We let the dogs sniff, and there seemed to be no problem, so Daniel let Koko loose. And they were off! Koko and Blondie raced around the yard in a free-for-all. Bandit stood in the center, confounded, looking like an old man, lost in traffic. He barked in consternation. He so much wanted to get a sniff, but he just couldn't keep up. Blondie was only about a third the size of Koko, but totally undaunted. They yapped and growled and screamed around the yard; the energy was tremendous. It was a joy to see Koko alive again. I shielded Bandit as best I could, from the swirling mass of dog flesh, as it roared by. He wanted so much to join in, but I knew he was no match for these two. I had become very protective of him, since his illness the summer before, and guarded him preciously—and he had no sense of his own. He voiced his displeasure, at being restrained.

I called Blondie over and fended Koko off, so Bandit could do some salutatory sniffing, but she was just too quick, and soon had him spinning in circles. Then Koko joined the fracas, and Bandit went down on his rear. I helped him up and led him away. "You better sit this one out," I told him.

Koko was untiring, stopping only once to spill the water on the ground, so she could take a drink, but Blondie was starting to fade. Koko chased her down relentlessly and soon Blondie sought refuge in the house. I took hold of Koko's leash, afraid now that the diversion was gone, her mind might drift back to escape, and we all trooped inside. We paid Blondie for her services in small, dog bones. She gobbled them down as fast as you could throw them. Eased by the presence of the other dogs, Koko waded through us, and milled around with the other two, though ever watchful for the slightest gesture in her direction. Clarrise kept, absentmindedly, reaching out for her, but Koko dodged her every time. We thought we might let the dogs have one more go round, but I decided we shouldn't press our luck: I had Koko on the leash now, and I wasn't too sure about letting her go again. One and one makes two, and Koko was starting to add things up.

I let Clarrise and Blondie out the front door. I thanked them for coming by. Clarrise said she could bring Blondie over again the next night, if I thought it was helpful, and I did. I was grateful for any diversion, and Koko sure needed one, plus the exercise. Once they were gone, we returned to the backyard for some post-event sniffing. Koko seemed calmer and wound down. She showed more interest in her immediate surroundings; I saw a flicker of light in her eyes.

That night began much calmer than the previous two. It had been a busy day, what with going to the vet, and then having Blondie over. Koko was already in her cave, asleep I presumed. We got ready for bed and turned off the lights. Bandit was already asleep on the floor. Then I heard her, pacing back and forth through the house, her nails clicking on the kitchen tile, and then on the plastic carpet runner by the front door. Back and forth, back and forth, she went. Daniel looked at me. Unwilling to repeat the performance of the night before, I thought to get a firm hand, right away. "Koko, no!" I said, and came charging out of the bedroom. I caught up to her in the kitchen, where struck by fear, she immediately squatted and urinated all over the floor. She looked up at me with eyes that grew even more fearful, once she realized what she had done. My heart immediately melted.

"Oh, Koko," I said. I felt awful, for coming down on her like that. She was so very sensitive. She was sure she had committed a capital offense, and stood cowering. I reached out to her slowly, so as not to frighten her, but could barely stroke the hair on her chest. I knew if I moved an inch in her direction, she would flee. "It's okay, baby," I told her, "it's okay. I'll just clean it up. No big deal." I got some paper towels, and calmly cleaned up the mess. She was not convinced and fled to her cave. I hated to leave her there like that, and decided it was time for Koko to come upstairs: she was spending way too much time in her seclusion, and that was accomplishing nothing.

I brought her up on a leash and got her to lie down beside the bed. Since our mattress was on the floor, we were at eye-level. I stroked her, hoping to soothe her to sleep. But it was all just too strange. Every time the furnace fired up, or the refrigerator kicked on, her head jerked up and she made a move to flee; but I held her firm. She was alarmed by every tick and creak the old house made. The final straw was the cats, as they began their midnight waltz upstairs, their dainty little paws sounded like hoofbeats on the ceiling. That did it! She was up and off to her cave. I let her go. I was just too tired to argue, or to explain to her about cats.

XXIV.
Just the Three Of Us

It was a short but restful sleep. I had gotten into the habit of rising even earlier than usual, since Koko came to stay, and with a new sense of responsibility. I had made a deep commitment to her. We had saved her life, in the physical sense, and I vowed to save her spirit as well: for without that, what was its value? I wanted to be there, ready and on-call, to help make the transition from freedom to captivity as painless as possible for her, for freedom, once gained, is a disastrous thing to lose. Fortunately, I had been fired from my most recent job the previous autumn (for saying out loud, that the king had no clothes) and I had all the time in the world for her.

The change had come in the blink of an eye and she was still reeling from the blow. She had no idea, how to exist in this new world, or even how to approach it. Her only response was to run and hide. I would have to draw her out and into it and teach her these new ways, how to "be" in this new world and where her place was. Not just to survive, but to thrive. It was a lot to learn. But before all that could begin, she had to trust me, and that seemed like a long way off. She was more feral than I thought, and to her senses, humans were poison and she was naturally repulsed. She was here only because I refused to let her go. I was her captor, nothing more. She was just doing what she had to do to survive.

I started the coffee to brew. By then Koko was standing on the landing, peeking at me around the corner. I never heard her come, but there she was. "Are you ready to go out?" I asked her, without looking at her. As soon as I did turn and see her, she scurried back down the stairs to her cave. I got the leash and followed her down. We went out to patrol the yard. I kept her in control and on the leash. She had learned just how long the leash was, and what maneuver would keep it just out of my reach. She could be very evasive, even in the confines of the yard. I just didn't feel like playing games this morning.

It was still dark outside and the world had barely begun to rise. The temperature held steady at twenty-above. It was peaceful and quiet. One by one, each at their own time, the neighbors left for work, leaving the neighborhood to us. We stood together in the yard and contemplated the new day. Bandit was already curled up in his straw fast asleep, unimpressed by the dawn about to break. When I decided the coffee was done, we headed in. I grabbed a covered cupful and we went back out. I thought Koko could use more outdoor time. She was spending way too much time in that dark hole. I set her loose, dragging the leash, and hung out by the rear fence, as sentry.

Koko roamed around the yard. She was content to be near Bandit, and constantly checked for his presence. She came to rely on him to be posted in his triangle, under the kitchen window, and if he wasn't there, could not be swayed until she located him. He was what bound us all together: he was the link, and a solid one, indeed. Sometimes I wonder if Bandit didn't just conjure her up, albeit begrudgingly, to provide for me, as if he could sense his own advancing age and eventual demise, knowing at what a loss I'll be without him, knowing it would take an extraordinary animal to replace him, and she certainly *was* that! But of course, that was just my fantasy-mind, entertaining absurdities. (And I also concocted a superstition, based on that fantasy, that the tamer and more of a companion *she* became, the more *he* would slip away from me—some kind of inverse cosmic equation—which caused me to view every progress she made with ambivalence. And in a way, that did happen, but it was just because he was getting old; he was getting very old.) Still, Bandit did seem to possess an inner wisdom, and sense of knowing, about the events that were taking place around him. He tolerated much more than I could have asked and showed a certain maturity, and security, in his position as alpha, unseen before. He wore the title nobly.

Koko learned from him, what was acceptable and not acceptable behavior in the household. She learned by watching. There was no going to the bathroom in the house, and the garbage can was definitely off limits. (Even with tempting chicken bones in it, it was never disturbed, except once by the neighbor cat, Jumper, and she almost got blamed. But when Jumper came strolling and squawking around the corner, I knew who the culprit was. He came and went freely, through the kitty-door, as if it was his own house. And we let him. He was old, and once had been a stray himself, but had taken up residence in the neighborhood, several years ago. I think it was Jumper who taught Koko her first lesson about cats, close-up, as one day she came sporting a gash on her nose.) She learned from Bandit, not to take food from our dinner plates, even when left unattended and within reach. (He would bark in consternation when that happened, with his nose just inches away, but not touching the food, as if to remind us that there was a meal going on here, and, let's get to it!) She learned that certain things in the house, such as the furniture, were not to be eaten, chewed upon, or torn apart. These were the basic ground rules, everything else was negotiable. And except for minor infractions, the rules remained unbroken. Bandit was a good teacher.

Daniel's work called that afternoon. He would be off for the east coast that night, with a load to Scranton. We had anticipated his leaving eventually, and had made some arrangements for getting him to work. I didn't want to leave Koko unattended and locked in the basement while I brought him there, fearful she might go berserk and injure herself somehow. Also, given enough time, I was afraid she might finally conquer the back door she had been trying so hard to claw and chew her way through. Clarrise had already offered to "baby-sit," in the event we both had to leave, so I took her up on the offer.

We left about nine-thirty, with Koko in the custody of Clarrise and Norman. I was like a new mother, going out for the first time, after the new arrival. I gave explicit instructions: Koko was in the basement. Unless there was a major ruckus, she was probably best left there. I thought she probably didn't need any more strange faces, peering at her. I had also been very careful not to deluge her with handling, for she still found my touch very strange, and I tried to convey to them, that it would be best, just to leave her alone. I was a little reticent to leave, but we had to go. And it actually felt good to be out.

Dealing with Koko the past several days had been pretty intense. She was so easily intimidated. Any careless word or action would send her scurrying away for her life. She was such a fragile spirit and had to be handled with thoughtfulness and gentle care. The damage one thoughtless moment could do, could take hours or days (or weeks) to repair. She needed constant praise and reassurance. I was very sensitive to her comfort and intruded on it as little as possible. Getting close to her would be a very gradual process. I hoped Clarrise and Norman would respect that. I was determined to make it back, fast.

Daniel climbed into his cab, reminding me to be careful and wishing me good luck. He had left the taming of Koko up to me, for obvious reasons. I could be with her more consistently and she seemed to be more at ease with me, probably because I was of the female gender. Daniel would be chasing a major snowstorm, all the way out to the east coast, and I advised him to take it easy the first leg, in order to give the storm a good headstart. But I knew he would overtake the snow, for his main mission in going out, was to return home as soon as humanly possible. The next few days would certainly be a trial for me I knew, but I assured him that I could handle it. Clarrise had offered to help out, by watching Koko while I walked Bandit, if necessary, or by bringing Blondie over to play. I was sure we would manage. When I returned to the house, Koko was huddled under the kitchen table, with Clarrise and Norman surrounding her.

"Was she throwing a fit?" I asked, as I entered the house, removing my jacket. Norman looked at a spot on the floor.

"Oh-no," Clarrise said, "I just heard her on the stairs, and thought she wanted to come up!" I assumed she just hadn't thoroughly understood my instructions. As soon as I opened the basement door, Koko made her exit and hurried back down to her cave.

We talked for a short while, but it was getting late and both of them had to work in the morning. Clarrise had been telling me about another dog they had found, and a neighbor's cat they had taken in, when its owner was sent to a nursing home. Sometimes they had as many as six dogs in the house, with her two, the strays she picked up off the street, and the dogs that belonged to her friends or relatives, who she baby-sat for. Norman was in charge of the cat population, and though they were strictly house-cats, he took them out religiously, each in turn, on leash and harness. Clarrise promised to check on me the next day, to see how I was doing, all alone. I thanked them sincerely for their help, and they were gone. The house was quiet.

The house always felt empty and suddenly quiet, with Daniel gone. But I loved the solitude and sank into it easily. I looked forward to this time alone. It was kind of nice sometimes, having the whole bed to myself, tapping to my own rhythms, doing what I wanted to do, when I wanted to do it, keeping to my own schedule (which yielded always and only, to Bandit's). Daniel and I had an unspoken agreement: if he would bring home the proverbial bacon, I would take care of everything else. I don't know if it was an equitable arrangement, but it assuaged my guilt, for not putting in a regular nine-to-five. And it seemed like there was always a myriad of things begging for my attention: mundane chores to be done, errands to run, home and vehicle maintenance, places to go, people to see, etc., etc., but when all of that was done, it freed me to my muses.

Music is the pastime that has sustained my creative fires through the years. It is something over which I offer to claim little control: it's just something I do and have done for years. With rhythm guitar, harmonica, and a voice that comes to me from out-of-the-blue, I have been known to jerk a tear or two. I claim no expertise, it is only my release. And although I have placed myself upon the public stage, it is a very unnerving thing for me to do: to let loose control and spill myself out, before stock random and unknowing eyes; to be suddenly so filled with emotion, as to feel on the brink of collapse. So mostly, it is a private and clandestine thing I do.

I used to reject the label Daniel placed on me: "You artists!" he would mutter and shake his head, at something I'd done or neglected to do. I always thought it to be a title reserved exclusively for the most prolific ones, made famous by their work, like Dylan or Van Gogh. Or in a broader sense, to me everybody was an artist, it was just a matter of practicing your specific talent. And that's what I did, when left to my own devices. And eventually, I accepted the label, and as with most labels people are given, used it as an excuse to explain my maladies in this existence, and my inability to go with the flow.

So I guess you could say I was one of those, born to the beat of a different drum. I am a non-conformist by nature, not by choice, though by intent and to some extent, a recluse. (I will be one of those people called eccentric, when I am old, I'm sure.) I notice everything, and even the smallest detail I take into account. I have a strong sense of fairness and probably take things too seriously; I like to see things out to their conclusion. I used to reject these proclivities in myself, but over the years, have come to embrace them. I seek out solitude now and rejoice in it. I have no excuses. And although I relish in my reclusivity, there is always a special air of excitement in the house the day Daniel is due home, and I welcome him back. And besides, I was never truly alone, for there was always Bandit—and now, there was Koko.

I was reluctant to take her out in the yard again, fearful to awaken the wild beast within, but she had been in the house for hours. Besides, Bandit needed to be rousted from his straw and brought in for the night, although he would stay stubbornly there if I allowed him to. But his old, arthritic bones really needed the relief of the warm house and soft bed, I thought, so we went out to get him.

Bandit was used to Daniel's comings and goings and was unaffected by it all. Koko, on the other hand, would be alarmed each time he returned, wondering who this strange person was in our kingdom, as if she was unable to remember him at all from time to time. (Don't feel bad, I would tell Daniel then, she does this to me nearly every, single morning!) Whatever progress we were making would come to a complete standstill when Daniel arrived: it was just one person too many for her to keep track of, and she would become all the more elusive and suspicious.

We three hung out in the backyard for awhile. It was nearing midnight. Koko stood in the middle of the yard listening: a dog barked far off, another answered. What was the message? I wondered. Koko raised her nose to the breeze, and I wondered what wondrous scents floated in on it. She observed the world silently, with every fiber of her being. She was totally aware. Bandit, on the other hand, noticed little, unless you had a leash in your hand or accidentally jangled the car keys. Then he was up like a shot. He could hear the Velcro being adjusted on your sneakers, from the backyard, through an open window, and would react to that, assuming it meant walk-time. He was sturdy and unflappable. He had navigated the crowded and noisy streets of the French Quarter in New Orleans, shortly after Mardi

Gras, even charming a hot dog and cup of water off of one of the street vendors. He knew his place in the scheme of things, and as long as I was beside him, he could handle anything.

I tried to reach out to Koko then, but her mind drifted elsewhere. Her head was full of the wild things: moonlit nights, chasing shadows at the river's edge, unchained and unbound. (I kept her secure on a leash that night, so she could not answer its call.) Even though the temperature was still in the 'teens, the cold began to gnaw at me and we were forced to head in. I rousted Bandit and led Koko inside.

Bandit headed directly for the bedroom, to resume his sleep. Koko paced back and forth through the house for what seemed like an eternity. Finally, I leashed her up and made her lie down beside the bed. I would have to force her into human contact, if she would not seek it herself. She was spending way too much time in the seclusion of her cave. She lay there, but nervous and fearful she was. Finally, I had soothed her enough that she drifted off.

She cried out and whimpered in her sleep. Her body flinched and her legs moved as if to run. I reached over and stroked her chest. She took my thumb in her mouth, absentmindedly, and gently began to suckle it, as if to nurse. You poor little baby, I thought, and once again, my eyes were wet, imagining all that she'd been through. I wondered, what terrible things had invaded her dreams, to make her cry out so? When I awoke the next morning, Koko was back in her cave, looking at me again, as if I was the strangest and most frightening creature she had ever seen.

XXV.
Wild Kingdom

There was nothing else I could do, but leave Koko shut in the basement, when I took Bandit out the next morning. It was the first time I had left her alone like that. She could hear Bandit's excited and frantic barking and clawed wildly at the kitchen door. I had decided to make it quick, but of course, Bandit had other ideas.

It was in the 'teens and he was in his element. He tried to tempt me toward the river but I was prepared for that and steered him into Dowling. He put off taking care of his business for as long as possible, but as soon as he did, I turned him toward home. (I hated to imagine, what was going on in the basement.) I walked with a sense of urgency, which Bandit must have picked up on, because he came along without too much protest, although he turned wistfully now and then, to glance at a yellow spot in the snow he had so wanted to sniff. "Come on, Bandit," I urged him, tugging on the leash.

When I returned, there were remnants of things torn up in the basement, but nothing of critical importance. (Koko would reveal an uncanny knack, for telling the difference between the two.) I could see she had done some major work on the back door, by the wood splinters lying all around, and there were some new gouges in the door to the kitchen. Fortunately, I had unplugged everything I could find in the basement, because she had ripped a power-strip surge protector off the wall and dismantled it, severing the cord. The only way she could have reached that, was by climbing up on the workbench, and then going up for it on her hind legs. No, it appeared Koko did not like to be confined. From then on, when I had to leave her (which was very seldom), I left rolled and crumpled up newspapers, stuck in strategic locations, for her to vent her frustrations on. They would always be shredded and torn to bits when I returned. Then Koko would peek out from behind the furnace, and I would scold her, "Oh, Koko, no, no," I would say, pretending that I cared. And then she was satisfied, thinking she had been *so* naughty!

Clarrise came by later that morning, to see how we were managing, just the three of us. I accepted her presence because she had been with it from the start, and she was always so willing to help—and I thought I needed help. She was really the only other person who knew the scope of what we were dealing with. We stood in the yard and watched the dogs, expounding theories and prospering solutions, when the phone rang.

"That's probably Daniel!" I said, and told Clarrise, "just try to stay between her and the back fence. I'll just be a minute."

I watched Clarrise and Koko through the kitchen window as I talked to Daniel. Clarrise was leaning over, saying something to Koko. Koko was several feet away, looking back at her over her shoulder warily. Suddenly, Clarrise swooped down and picked up the end of the leash Koko was dragging and began pulling Koko toward her. Koko was startled and panicked. Then they disappeared behind the big maple. I told Daniel what was happening, over the phone. "I'd better get out there," I said, and he agreed. We hung up abruptly.

I went out to rescue Koko. I didn't confront Clarrise on her behavior, assuming she meant no harm and feeling so much like the over-protective parent. Whatever the damage, it had already been done. From then on, it would be next to impossible to catch Koko once she was loose in the yard, even with the twelve-foot leash dragging behind her. She was tired of getting caught, and then being forced to go where she didn't want to go, and to do things she didn't care to do. She was used to being her own boss. And she had the remedy. She simply went to the most secluded area of the yard, out of my view, and in a matter of a minute or so, chewed the leash off, leaving only the chrome snap and a shredded stub of nylon still hooked onto the harness. She had moved herself adroitly out of check, and she was *very* proud. Well, there went twelve bucks, I thought. And it wouldn't be the last time, either.

If you did let Koko loose in the yard, dragging a leash, you had to keep her moving and on her feet, or she would simply chew it off. I still didn't dare leave her in the yard, totally unsupervised because, though she showed no motivation to jump, I knew she easily could, and if something on the outside threatened her enough, she might. And luring her into the basement when I had to leave was becoming harder and harder. I had used every trick I could think of, to get her down there. Each ploy worked only once (she was *very* shrewd) and I was running out of ideas. So most of the time, Koko stayed on a leash.

The situation was improved when Daniel returned. He could stay with Koko while I took Bandit, and she didn't have to be locked anywhere. Then Bandit and I could enjoy our walk, unhurried, knowing Koko was supervised. We even made it to the river, and Bandit was joyful. I felt bad for depriving him, and was determined that this undertaking with Koko would not be at his expense. Sometimes, it was a hard promise to keep.

Koko had been with us for almost two weeks. As January left and February rolled in, the temperature sank again into the twenty-below range, to remind us that winter was still with us as well. I was glad to have Koko in out of the elements, though she was hardly any tamer than she had been when we first found her. She had to be forced into any contact and then she only tolerated it, eager to get away. She could only be approached when tucked away in her cave. She had pretty much accepted the confines of the yard as her domain, and was content to stay, but only as long as she could set the rules of engagement. If she felt threatened enough, I'm sure she could have flown over that fence in a second—even the meter-reader could have provided that stimulus. So when Koko was loose in the yard, I kept a watchful eye.

It was very tiring and I was exhausted, trying to stay one step ahead of her and always one step behind Bandit. I could have easily put her on the heavy chain, and kept her tied to the wash-pole, but I refused to do that. It would have broken every promise I had made to her. She could never be happy like that, and I would not betray her. She would have her freedom, but within certain bounds. For freedom, in a civilized society, came in degrees and with certain limits and responsibilities. And freedom wields a two-edged sword. Had she really been free at the river? Perhaps in some ways, but certainly not in others. To paraphrase a line by Bob Dylan, even birds are bound by the limits of the sky. I would teach her a new way of freedom, and hopefully, she could flourish in it and be happy—happier than she had been before, that was my goal. But in order to give her her freedom, I would first have to take it all away. That became more and more evident, as time went on.

And so we muddled through, and Daniel was off again. He would be heading to the southeast, to the Raleigh-Durham area. At least the weather would be more hospitable there. Our nights were below-zero again and the days, only in the single digits. If the groundhog saw its shadow, promising six more weeks of winter, that was just fine. Because for us here, in Minnesota, the promise of six more weeks of winter was nothing, if not a blessing. But we all knew better. We should be so lucky to have it over that fast!

Koko was getting worse instead of better, playing hard-to-get, once she was loose in the yard. I was tired and frustrated, trying to give her some freedom, while still keeping tabs on her. Finally, it got to the point where I decided, if she jumped, she jumped, and I would just have to take that chance. I couldn't do it anymore. But I prepared myself for that possibility and decided, if she escaped, first, I would sleep for a couple of days, then go and retrieve her and start all over again. There was no doubt in my mind that she would return to that place at the river.

Koko continued to destroy the back door whenever she was confined to the basement. I only left her to take Bandit for his walks, or when I had to bring Daniel to work or pick him up, but that was enough. Something needed to be done. There was an old wooden, accordion-style child's-gate that stretched across the landing to the basement stairs, put there by the previous owners. Though by itself it was of little value (she could easily have demolished it in seconds) I thought if I used it for a foundation, and faced it off with some of that four-foot high wire-fence we had leftover from the back fence, it might at least keep her away from the back door. I set about working on my project. Koko watched with interest. I left the storm-door propped open so she could see. She was very timid about coming into the house on her own accord, and though it didn't do much for our heating bill, we often left the back door propped open, so if the mood struck her, she could come in. The house was always cold anyway, and the furnace ran constantly, so it really didn't make that much difference. The kitchen was freezing, but the front of the house was comparatively warm.

"This is to keep that mean, old furnace-monster downstairs," I declared to her, as I constructed my latest deterrent, which was really, to keep *her* down there. The furnace had become, and would remain forever, a bane to her existence. For whatever reason, whenever the furnace flared, she would quit whatever she was doing, or rise if she was sleeping, and head outside. It was very Pavlovian. My only guess is that when she was collapsed there in her cave in the basement, those first couple of days, she must have found the furnace a scary and awesome thing. And I suppose it could sound rather intimidating, as the ignition clicked, then the gas came hissing out, and the *whoosh!* as the burners fired up, but you would think eventually, she would get over it. But she never did. And it was a sorry situation, because in this climate the furnace was on for at *least* six months out of the year, and during that time, the Furnace Monster ruled, and she relegated herself to the out-of-doors, even when it was twenty and thirty-below. Then it was a hard thing to watch, as she huddled in her straw, braced against the elements (she refused to use the house we built for her), but there was nothing I could do: I knew if I tried to approach her she would simply jump up and flee; I just had to tell myself, she knows how to survive.

I continued to construct my defense at the top of the stairs, while Koko looked on, scolding the Furnace Monster for "scaring my poor Koko." Koko's fears were surmounted only by her inquisitiveness and she watched the action with full intent. And I watched her out of the corner of my eye. Her face was most expressive and it was a delight to watch the changes that passed there, and her postures. She would bob her head up and down, between her front legs, studying, studying. Her neck and body seemed disconnected, and moved and craned in mysterious ways. She could crane her neck all the way around, with her body in a horseshoe shape, and look back out over her tail, with the greatest of ease. Her eyes saw everywhere, all at once, and what her eyes couldn't see, her ears could hear, or her nose could smell. She could react so fast, she could be in five different places all at once, then back in her original position, and you would never actually see her move. She was at *least* as fast as lightning. But her confused and perplexed look was the most comical, and it didn't take much to elicit that.

Koko was very mindful of how things were, where they belonged, and any subtle change in that set-up. If she did dare to venture into the house, and so much as a pair of boots was out of place (perhaps they had been shucked and left by the stove, instead of being put in their usual place, on the mat by the back door), that would be enough to stop her and send her scurrying back out into the yard, to puzzle on it and decide how this change might affect her existence. She was very paranoid about change. Heaven forbid, we should get new furniture, or you decided to wear the red windbreaker, instead of the gray jean-jacket! She would be sure it was some kind of trick, and that you were threatening her very survival.

I put my iron defense to the test when I walked Bandit the next morning. I never even considered trying to walk them both. Bandit was a handful by himself, and it was hard enough, having to climb over snowbanks and navigating the icy walks with just him, I couldn't imagine taking them both. Koko was too unpredictable, and you just never knew what was going to set her off. Then it was all I could do just to get her home safely, and I could just imagine Bandit, dragging along behind. No, for now, Koko would have to stay in the basement. We left her there and headed out. Bandit was stubborn and would not be hurried. When we did return, it appeared my defense had held, and for once the back door was unscathed. But there were big gouges in the round, wooden handrail that ran up the stairs, made by some very large and determined canine teeth. And the top of the wire was bent over, but she had not been able to defeat the obstacle. Check and mate! I thought haughtily. But inside, I knew the game had barely begun.

Basically, what we had was a wild animal running around the backyard. I could not approach her, and she certainly wasn't going to approach me. It seemed we were making no progress, as far as domesticating her was concerned, and we were headed for a stalemate. How could I show her that I wasn't going to harm her, when I couldn't even get *near* her? This question would plague and perplex me for many sleepless nights to come. It was a real paradox. I didn't want to totally confine her (although it seemed to be coming to that), and thereby, defeat her, for then our relationship would simply be one of captor and captive, and her nature would demand that she constantly seek to escape. Neither one of us could be happy, under those terms. There had to be some common ground between us somewhere, but the only ground between us now was the backyard, as we stood in separate corners and sized each other up. My intent was to "catch her," and hers, was not to be caught: it would be a test of will and wit. We lived in a fragile and curious state of co-existence, nothing more. We lived in two separate worlds, and it seemed, that never the twain shall meet.

Koko always rested easier at night, after a play-session with Blondie. That afforded me some relief. But usually by the middle of the night, she would be up and pacing, maybe in response to the flaring of the furnace. Usually, she would eventually retire back to her cave, but if she didn't, I would get up and take her outside for awhile, on the leash. Then I would be up before the dawn. Bandit pretty much ignored the goings-on around him, and only grumped and grumbled if his sleep was disturbed. He got tired of me, using him to lure Koko here or there, but would do so, though begrudgingly and with protest; sometimes, it was the only way.

I started to discourage friends from dropping by. Koko was terrified if someone arrived unexpectedly, and would begin eyeing the fence for a way out. But the lack of company suited me just fine, and she gave me an excuse to indulge in my reclusive behavior. "You can't let that animal run your life!" one of my friends admonished me, and I felt very defensive, until I realized that I could if I chose to, for that was the right of majority. People, I thought, just didn't understand.

I made the mistake of letting Koko out into the yard one morning, unrestrained. When it came time for Bandit's walk, I could neither tempt her into the basement or get a hold of her in the yard. Bandit was frantic to be on his way, and the more I tried to accost her, the more suspicious she became, and the more consternated Bandit became, until the situation escalated into one of sheer frustration. Finally, there was no recourse but to leave her there in the yard. She stood on Bandit's doghouse and watched in through the kitchen window as I led Bandit into the front room, out of her view, to hook him up. We slipped quickly (though not so quietly) out the front door. I was hoping we could get back before she realized we were gone, or at least, before she decided what to do about it. I just prayed that she would still be there when we returned; and miraculously, she was.

She greeted Bandit as if he had been gone for days to distant and dangerous lands, though it had barely been fifteen minutes. She crawled up to him on her belly and whimpered and whined almost inaudibly, as she licked in his mouth and poked him with her nose. She slapped him with her big paw and tried to lay it over his shoulder. He ducked and dodged her assault, but he was no match for her enthusiasm, and soon sought refuge in his house, complaining loudly all the way. (He had always been an island.) But Koko didn't seem to mind. She was just glad to have him back. She just loved him, any way he came.

XXVI.
The Great Escape

The next morning, the same thing—almost. Koko was loose in the backyard and would not be caught; Bandit was raring to go. I left her in the yard again, but knew that I was pressing my luck. She knew the routine now, and that Bandit's frantic barking meant we would be leaving her. She clawed frantically on the back storm-door; I could hear her claws, scraping on the window glass. I made a mental note: we would have to put some plywood up there, lest she go right through it and sever a limb. But we had to go.

We slipped out the front door. I was feeling very uneasy at leaving her there, but there wasn't much else to do. I was determined to make it back fast. We headed west, just one block, then north two, then headed east for two blocks, returning on the sidewalk opposite the Dowling yard. Bandit wished to go there, but I kept him on the other side of the street. He could burn up a lot of minutes, snuffling around at Dowling, and I felt a sense of immediacy, that we'd better get back. As Bandit investigated an invisible scent in the snow, I glanced up, to see how far yet to the corner, tugging at the leash impatiently. I couldn't believe my eyes! Koko was on the loose! She was running down the middle of the street, heading east, toward the river! Her body was in a crouching position and her tail was tucked and down. She looked nervously from side to side. She was running scared.

"Koko!" I shouted, and tore off my glove, to let go a shrill whistle. Her head shot up and she spun around. She came bounding toward us through the snow, her face had turned into a grin. She bounced and bounded around Bandit with obvious delight. I didn't flatter myself: it was him she had come to find. We headed directly home and she followed us easily. She stuttered a little, at the gate, but soon was back in the confines of the yard; I closed it behind her. Well, now I knew for sure she could jump the fence. I looked around, wondering where exactly she had gone over. My first instinct was to immediately put her back on a leash and get her in control, but I stopped myself. She had chosen to come back: it was a good sign. Even though she showed no special propensity toward me, it seemed she had found herself a home. One threshhold had been crossed. And in a few more days, another mountain would be moved. For the first time, Koko drank water from a bowl.

She dipped her face into the bowl hesitantly, unsure of exactly how to approach this new concept, water-from-a-bowl. She adjusted herself, trying to get the distance right (in relation to the length of her tongue), lapping at thin air, or accidentally dipping her nose into the water too far. But finally, she got it right and drank, though haltingly. Her eyes darted suspiciously, studying the interior of the bowl, for any sign of trickery. From that day forward, she always took her water from a bowl (although she still liked to spill it out onto the ground occasionally, to poke at the little rivers of water as they trickled down their paths). It had been a wearisome three weeks, just to reach *this* level of domesticity. Then I knew it was going to be a long haul, and I was in it for the duration.

I fooled myself into thinking that Koko was becoming much more cooperative, but it was just because she was always on a leash. Once she was loose in the yard, she was as wild as ever. The more freedom I granted, the more she used it up. She was completely out-of-control. She would not be caught, and when I finally did get a hold of her, I hated to let her go. I could usually round her up, if she was dragging a leash, but that had already been defeated by her (we now had several leashes, with no snap-hooks on the other end). I thought I had a new fool-proof solution.

I went to the neighborhood hardware store and bought a fourteen-foot length of lightweight chain. I attached a snap-hook to one end of it (leftover from one of the many leashes she had devoured), but didn't attach the other end to anything. I hooked it onto the faded, orange nylon-harness she wore. I still wanted her to have some measure of freedom, to roam the yard, but now she would be dragging the chain. And I would have something to aim for, when she needed to be caught—something she couldn't chew off. Check! I thought again. And Koko knew she was caught.

She slumped around the yard, looking forlorn and forsaken. She eyed me warily and kept her distance. It occurred to me, that she just might have been on a chain some time previously. She knew just how to step over it, and keep aside from it, so she wouldn't get her legs all tangled up—but who could ever say for sure. She looked so defeated. I hated to see her that way, but I didn't know what else to do. Although there were other suggestions.

Daniel was at his wit's end, too. He thought I was spending way too much time, out in the elements, pursuing after this beast. To him, it seemed an impossible task, and he was ready to invest in a kennel, pointing out to me in the yard, exactly where we could put it. He was ready to give in. But the whole idea reeked of failure to me, and most of all, how it would fail Koko. I adamantly resisted, and pleaded for more time. I knew once she was put in a kennel, that would be her life, and I just couldn't do it. Let's wait and see, I begged, just a while longer. Clarrise had a solution too, as we stood in the backyard, Koko completely out of reach as usual, eyeing us suspiciously. "Well," she said, "if the animal just can't bond, then the only humane thing to do, would be to put her to sleep. . . ." I rose up inside and bristled, but said nothing. It would *never* come to that, I knew. Something was growing between us, and though still awkward and unsure, it was there; I could sense it.

Now, dragging the chain, Koko was mine whenever I wanted her, and she knew it. But still she was a challenge to catch. Sometimes I would go out into the yard and accost her, just to show her I could. She would always flee. Then I would have to maintain my pursuit until she was caught, or she would forever think she could run from me. At the deciding moment, when she knew I had her, as I reached out to take hold of the chain, she would squat and urinate, and a look of fear would race through her eyes. Then I would take the end of the chain and ease up to her, complimenting her for being such a good girl and assuring her that I wasn't going to hurt her. I would pet her and fondle her and rub her chest, trying to get her to loosen up. Once she accepted my contact and relaxed, I would let her go. Over the course of a day, she could become quite tame, and sometimes she even allowed me to approach her in the yard, although fearful she was and her body flinched as if to run. But she had the chain on, and perhaps she knew I would eventually catch her anyway. Then I would pet her and congratulate her enthusiastically on her progress. But any progress we made would be stolen away during the night, and we would start again from scratch the next morning, with her looking at me as if I was the most dreadful creature she had ever seen. She was sure that *this* time, I had come to do her in. And I was beginning to take offense, at her inability to trust me, for I had been falsely accused—but I had no resource to argue my case. It was very frustrating. I just wanted her to like me.

One day, my friend Margaret called. She needed my help. She was an elderly lady I had met through a friend I was working for one summer, doing minor home repairs, painting, and other assorted tasks. I had done some work for her previously, and we had really hit it off. She asked if she could call on me in the future, and I agreed. From there, a firm friendship formed.

She was a child survivor of the polio epidemic that swept through the Twin Cities in 1916. She was now confined to a wheelchair and, since her husband had died several years earlier, was completely on her own. She was very strong-minded about her independence. She had a cheerful and radiant personality, in spite of all her hardships, and never complained. She was generous and forthright—an inspiration. When she called, I responded as best I could. A severe case of the flu that winter, which complicated existing health problems, had put her in a bad way (and eventually would land her on death's doorstep, but of course I didn't know that at that time). She needed my help for some basic tasks. I was happy to oblige.

I had left Koko in the yard before, on a couple of occasions, when I knew I would only be gone for a short while. I had taken to parking the car out in front. I would slip quietly and unnoticed out the front door, as Koko exhibited anxiety and a desire to take after the car, whenever I left. She had the faded, orange harness on and the long chain dragging. I was pretty sure she wouldn't try to jump the fence in that attire, but if she did, and got hung up, well, I thought, she could just hang there until I got back. Margaret needed me. She knew of my plight with Koko, and being a dog-lover herself, was always interested to hear. And though I might have been a little hasty in my tasks, and anxious to leave, Margaret understood.

My heart was always a little in my throat, whenever I returned after being gone, wondering what I would find—or not find. But Koko was still there. She was stuck away in the corner of the yard, where the house and fence provided a neat enclave, about six feet deep. This is where, in the yard, she ran to, to hide or to be "caught." I was glad to see her and was relieved, though momentarily. Koko looked up at me with apprehension in her wondering eyes. As I looked more closely, I noticed little bits of orange scattered around her. The chain was lying a few feet away, still attached to the harness that Koko was no longer wearing. Since she couldn't get the chain off the harness, she simply got the harness off altogether. She had chewed it to smithereens; one strap still lay across her back, secured to nothing. A little overkill, don't you think? I could have said, but said instead, "Oh, Koko, what have you done?" She ran to the other corner of the yard, looking guilty, but satisfied. She had made her move and I had to rethink my strategy. For now, Koko was on the loose and beyond any control; and she knew it.

Koko could neither be caught or tempted into the basement. She had her freedom, though little it was, and was not about to surrender it. I decided to leave her be and have Clarrise come by later with Blondie. I knew that with that diversion, I would be able to grab hold of her collar. And when I did finally get a hold of her, I made my next move.

I removed the choke-collar she always wore, and buckled an old, blue strap collar that had been Bandit's, tightly (but not too tightly) around her neck. I attached the length of chain to that. She couldn't reach it to chew through it, and she couldn't chew through the chain. Once again, she was caught. But this time, totally. It was check and mate. She slunk around the yard, looking totally oppressed. It was a sorry sight, but it had to be done. I would have to take all her freedom away, and give it back to her gradually and in pieces; she would have to earn it. And each small freedom that was granted, would be done by my own hand, until she no longer saw me as her captor, but as her liberator.

XXVII.
Walking the Dog

It was always easier to manage when Daniel was home. He could stay and dissuade Koko from jumping the fence, while I walked Bandit. But when he was gone, it was always a quandary, what to do, what to do. Koko either had to be lured and locked into the basement (which was becoming an impossible task) or brought along. I knew if I left her alone in the yard she would surmount the fence and come searching for us, and she might find something else, totally unexpected; it could be a real disaster. But convincing her to come along was not always the easiest thing to do.

She wanted to come, but not if it meant being on a leash and in my control. She wanted to run under people's windows and hide in the bushes and dart across streets, like some kind of wild wolf-dog. It took months upon months of my pleading with her (with Bandit throwing a fit in the background the whole time, frantic to be on his way) to finally convince her that she could only leave the yard under that restraint. It was an impossible situation. When she did allow me to hook her up for a walk, she walked well beside me, taking up naturally on my left. (Bandit had always heeled to the right and I found it peculiar that Koko so staunchly chose the other side.) If a situation arose and she wound up on my right side, she would react in an exaggerated fearful and cowering manner and look up at me as if I was apt to release a blow. Then she would make her way quickly, back to my left side, where she seemed to be less distressed. So it worked out well, in that regard, and kept us from being constantly entangled. I could never figure out that particular aversion of hers (Clarrise thought she might have bad vision on that one side), and she would exhibit many other symptoms, that could be construed as clues; although clues to what, I'm not sure.

Koko had a special aversion to pick-up trucks, especially ones with toppers. She didn't like vehicles with tinted windows and people with sunglasses on made her especially nervous. We would cross the street and walk on the other side, rather than face any of these obstacles. Though all people frightened her, she was especially afraid of young, adolescent males, and even more-so, if they were in hooded sweatshirts. She may have run into some of these young, punk-gangsters down at the river. Perhaps they even chased and tormented her, or threw stones at her. Who could tell, with their brute mentality? A person approaching from behind, although blocks away, would always put her into a spin, scooting ahead with her tail plastered between her legs, glancing back over her shoulder, sure the marauder was intent upon her. When that happened, it was all I could do to hold her back, and keep from dragging Bandit along, who often had his nose buried in some irresistible scent, totally unaware of the drama being played out around him. He would always look up at me questioningly, and react stubbornly, as all of a sudden, we would have to cross the street. We *never* cross here, he would look at me as if to say, we *always* cross over *there*. We called him "Rain-dog," so stuck in his ways and methodical he was on his walks. But one day, even he would give up his well-worn patterns, to accommodate Koko's neuroses.

We were a regular comedy team, the three of us, each with our own agenda. They were Yin and Yang. Bandit was totally oblivious to any evil or danger in the world, Koko saw it everywhere. He was staunch and dependable, she was flighty and unpredictable. He was bold and demanding, she was timid and fearful. And I think other dogs could sense her apprehension, and her not-belonging, as we strode through their neighborhoods. A phenomenon occurred which I had never seen before, as dogs would come to attack and dominate her, even from the confines of their yards. One, who had never been known to do it before, jumped over his fence and came charging toward Koko. Bandit and Daniel bravely stepped in while we made our escape.

Another very small dog (commonly referred to as an "ankle-biter") came ripping out of its yard, and lit into the terrified and cowering Koko. The animal weighed, maybe, all of six pounds. She had no confidence as it was, and on a leash she had even less: she felt helpless and totally vulnerable.

Every walk was an adventure. Each time we arrived home, safe and unscathed, was a success, and I felt relieved. When Daniel was gone, I enlisted the help of Clarrise, which she had so generously offered, although in hindsight and in the long run, she may have been more of a hindrance than a help. She was always reaching out to touch Koko, anytime she came near, which made Koko feel even more paranoid and vulnerable about being on the leash, and Koko was constantly trying to dodge her. I bit my tongue, because Clarrise had been so gracious to help, but made a concerted effort to keep Koko clear of her ever-reaching grasp. Couldn't she see how uneasy it made her?

Clarrise had often offered to take Bandit with her, when her and her "pup club" went to the river in the morning, to relieve me of walking him, so I could stay with Koko. She had also offered, that her and Norman could come by and take Koko out, to give me a break, and to give Koko some more and much needed exercise. But I always declined: Bandit was hard enough for *me* to keep track of, and I knew all of his tricks. And with the number of dogs she was toting, I knew he would be lost for certain. And as for Koko, she didn't care to go anywhere without Bandit. No, we were a threesome now, and somehow we would manage. (She seemed so overly anxious to get away with one of the dogs, it made me wonder why.) But I allowed her to accompany us on our walks, her taking Bandit, and me, with Koko.

I watched their every move. With his advancing age, sometimes you had to be Bandit's eyes. He might stumble unexpectedly and had a tendency to blunder his way into predicaments. Once he got his nose stuck in a scent, you had to be forceful but gentle, pulling him out, or he would wind up sprawled on the ground: his front end was strong, as was his will, but his posterior was weak. I urged Clarrise to take care. Especially when we reached the parkway, I warned her to hold him up tight.

Bandit had never mastered the art of crossing the street; his strategy was just the opposite of what it should have been. When the coast was clear, he refused to budge, his nose stuck stubbornly in a scent. But as soon as a car approached, you could see him getting ready to launch. I assumed he went by sound, because as soon as the car was upon us, without looking up at all, he would make his move and suddenly decide to go, darting out at exactly the wrong time, putting himself directly in the path of the oncoming car. I warned Clarrise, and when he actually did it, she was still surprised, and barely stopped his forward progress in time. I held my breath. She squealed with laughter.

"You weren't kidding, were you!" she said, and began explaining to Bandit, in a mock, scolding voice, the proper way to cross a street.

"It's no use," I told her and explained, "I've been trying to teach him that for twelve years. He just doesn't get it!" No, I decided (what I had already suspected), there was no way these two would ever be allowed out of my sight. I knew Bandit's bag of tricks so well: we had walked together for many miles, for many years.

There is a certain sub-culture that exists in a city such as this, guided by its own customs and mores and rules of etiquette. It is a society of dog-walkers, who prowl the streets in the early morning and late evening. Some people, you could set your watch by. They were the regulars, and appeared on their well established routes, at a certain and specific time each day. Others were more random entities, who you might cross paths with sporadically. People were known, not by their names, but by their dog's name.

Most people were cordial, and allowed their dogs to meet and greet; the chatter between the humans usually centered on the dogs. Some people avoided contact altogether, and would not even say hello; and they were respected in their solitude. You got to know who was who, and acted accordingly. If a person was unfriendly, you could bet their dog probably was too, and you kept your distance. Bandit thought he was some kind of goodwill ambassador, and when he was off the leash, had no qualms about running up to a strange dog to say hello. He had not an aggressive bone in his body, although he had been put down by other dogs more than once. I could usually anticipate his flight, and get a hold of him, but sometimes I missed. Most people understood, and when I called ahead to tell them, he was fine, they let go this breech in etiquette. But some people took dire offense, and would comment, under their breath, something about me not being able to control my dog. Then I would tell them not to worry about it, and off we would run. The next time we met, I would be sure to have Bandit under control.

Most dogs did well to meet with the least human involvement. There was less posturing. When strange dogs met (unless one was unusually aggressive), it was better just to stay out of it and let them work it out. As soon as an owner stepped in, the dog's reaction was to become even more protective and aggressive. If we met a dog on the loose, and the owner started scrambling to get him under control, I would call ahead and assure them that it was all right to leave him free. Then I would stand aside and let the dogs meet on their own terms. There is a leash law in this city, by which we all must abide. But there are certain places too, where it is common knowledge, that there will be dogs running free, favorite haunts at the river, especially at Thirty-sixth Street and on the lower path. For there is nothing more satisfying and joyful to see then a dog running free, being a dog. And although you risked the wrath of the Park Patrol, and might even get a ticket, it was worth the price. Newcomers to the area, who might not know, soon learned that in the early morning and evening, certain places were given over to the dogs. If that was not satisfactory, then those people would find somewhere else to go.

I have watched dogs on the trail grow old and feeble, until one day, they appear no more. And then too, neither does the owner who has (by the loss) also given up their membership in this exclusive club. So I have pictured myself one day, sitting on a bench overlooking the river, a hole in my heart and an empty leash in my hand, staring blankly across; and I dread that day to come. But always in the spring, new puppies appear on the scene, and new dogs come, and the cycle begins again. It is to this place that Koko would make her debut. I thought it was time for her to revisit the river, though we would not return to that specific place on the hill where we found her—not yet, anyway.

Koko wasn't at all impressed to be back at the river. I thought it would be a happy homecoming for her, but she was more fearful and nervous than ever, as if there were too many unsettling memories there. We walked the lower path, which was especially narrow in the winter. The simple sound of my footsteps behind her unnerved her so (they rang in her head as pursuit), that I kept her alongside or behind me. If we met any people on the trail, with or without dogs, she would bolt up the hill and stand in the trees, terrified. I would go stand beside her, and try to calm her, and tell her to stay. I would place myself between her and the offenders, and act as her protector.

It is amazing how many people recognized her. Many just stood with their mouths gaping open and their eyes wide with disbelief, stuttering, "Isn't that . . . ? Isn't that . . . ?" and I would assure them that it was. Then I would repeat again, briefly, the story of how she was caught, and they would express their relief and delight that the animal had a good home. They could see the wildness in her, and were grateful to me, for having the nerve to tackle it. And I couldn't explain to them, that I hadn't chosen to do it, but was possessed to do it. Koko would look increasingly uneasy, the longer the conversation ran, with the eyes of the strangers upon her, making her cringe. She was vulnerable on the leash, and unable to flee, and her intense fear would register in me, and we would have to be on our way. Koko was always glad to get home. Each time I removed the leash from her, and let her go, in her mind, I was setting her "free," and she was grateful to me for that.

Koko met different people with varying degrees of wariness. One woman we met at the river, with a dog of her own, stopped to talk, having recognized Koko. She seemed like a nice lady, and perfectly harmless, but I could feel a deep and low growl emanating from Koko's throat. It was inaudible to the person I was talking to, and made me wonder what she sensed that had elicited such a response. Some people she almost tolerated, and although she still fled up the hill to stand in the trees, I could tell she was less bothered. Some people she showed a real aversion to, and then she was completely out of control, and it was all I could do, just to get us home safely. It is that sixth-sense, that we humans lack, that told her about people. And although her reactions were always over-amplified, I trusted her instincts, and my gut-feeling was often the same, if I really listened. It was something to do with karma.

As spring rolled around and people emerged from their winter seclusion, to hang out on their stoops, or in their yards, Koko started to refuse to walk the neighborhood streets. I could force her to, but it was always a nightmare for her, and so, a nightmare for me. We began to take our walks very early in the morning, or in the evening, when the people were less. I thought we might take the opportunity to try and get her accustomed to riding in the car, so we could go to less frequented places, where human contact would be minimal. Each time, I had to drag her to the car and force her in, then drag her out when we got to a place, then drag her to the car again, when it was time to leave. I thought eventually, she would come to like the outings, but even after a couple of dozen tries, she never did. In fact, she found no joy in them at all, and eventually I abandoned the whole idea. It was just too much work, and no fun for anyone—except Bandit, of course, he was always ready to go.

Soon, the river got to be too much for her too, as people came out in droves, on bikes and in-line skates and jogging, until the only place she would willingly go was to Dowling. There, if people were about, she could hide in the trees and watch from a distance; if we could stay far enough afield from any humanity, she could tolerate being out. Koko was a homebody, and she would have preferred, just as well, to stay in the yard. She went out only to be near Bandit, and because I made her. I thought it might do her some good.

XXVIII.
Romantic Interlude

One day, I could stand it no longer: the time was ripe. Koko had been with us for over a month. She seemed to recognize us as her pack, and though she was still very elusive, a fragile truce had developed. And the animal really needed to run; she just needed to cut loose. She had been under my constant control and supervision, and we were both worn out from it. The snow was considerable, and the paths were awkward. I could not even begin to move fast enough, to give her any kind of a work-out. It was a very early Saturday morning. The streets were empty and the city was silent. We entered Dowling by the nearest gate. I could feel her yearning, and it was my own.

"I'm gonna let her go," I told Daniel. My heart was pounding and in my throat. He urged me to do it. He had no apprehension, though mine was strong. The trite old adage, if you love something let it go; if it comes back to you, it's yours. If not, it never was, floated through my mind, and though the anxiety coursed through me, I leaned over and removed the leash from Koko's harness. She looked at me in disbelief, then took off at the speed of light, across the field. Looking back over her shoulder, she appeared to be laughing. Her eyes were rank with excitement. In seconds she was out of sight. She flew as if above the ground; and we called her, Runs on the Wind.

I whistled for her and she came galloping back, but not too close. She stood in the trees and accounted for Bandit. Then she was off again. She drank her freedom ferociously, and it was a joyful thing to behold, but scary in its abandon. I knew it would be useless to try and catch her. She would have to follow us home, much like she did on that first day. And she did, though she was wary of coming through the gate, and it took several tries to finally get her in; and then it was only by her devotion to Bandit, and the lure of irresistible treats, that she came.

I let her go several times thereafter. But each time, she was harder and harder to round up; she was becoming more confident in her freedom, and bolder. One day, I let her go prematurely, before I had completely surveyed the grounds. I never noticed the elderly lady and her poodle-dog across the way. But Koko did, and off she flew. I knew it was useless to call her. I held my breath. Koko went over the rise, and disappeared from view. I could only imagine the scene that was being played out there. There was nothing else to do but turn around and head in the exact opposite direction. I knew Koko would eventually follow us, but for now, I didn't want to know her. Yes, I denied her. When Koko finally did come, we hurried home. And as always, it was a challenge to coax her back into the yard, once we got there.

Koko was definitely a loose cannon out there and beyond any control. It soon became apparent that she just couldn't run free anymore. One morning, she ran down a jogger, although as soon as the woman turned around and confronted her, Koko fled. But she was an awesome sight, coming at you, if you didn't know her, and I didn't want to be responsible for any person's heart attack. And it was bad public relations. I decided, first, she would have to learn to walk *on* a leash, then she could be let off; but foremost, she had to relinquish her intense fear of "being caught." Once she was free, she was every bit as wild and elusive as she had been at the river. Only now, she called another place home.

One day, late in February, Bandit suddenly began to take a keen interest in Koko. I watched her as she flicked her tail at him and rubbed herself provocatively along the length of the fence, a sly look in her eye. Then I thought of the strange dogs I had to shoo away from the fence, in recent nights. And I may be slow, but it finally occurred to me, that Koko was going into heat. I had no experience at all with female dogs (ours had always been males), and I wasn't sure what it all entailed, but I knew we were in for a ride. Clarrise would know, I thought, she had a female dog. And she agreed, Koko was probably going into her first heat.

There were no outward signs of it, except for Bandit's behavior, but I knew from the start, eventually she would have to be spayed. And even though I hated to put her through another trip to the doctor's office, this was as good a time as any. It was Friday, and we would bring her in on Monday. The vet-tech lady patiently reminded me not to feed her the day before.

I was a little concerned for Bandit's safety. I knew that a female in heat could attract lovelorn dogs from miles around. And the snowbank on the outside of the back fence was pretty high up there, and if some roving stud did happen to get into the yard, it could be a fight to the finish. And Bandit would definitely come out the loser; he was defenseless, under attack. But as usual, Bandit turned out to be his own worst enemy.

Bandit pursued her relentlessly throughout the weekend. And she was no help. She ate up his attention. She was having a game of it. She teased and provoked him. Then just when he was about to make his move, she would dart off, leaving him with nothing but the empty air. He would try to mount her again, but his rear legs would give out, and he would end up, sprawled on the ground. He was unrelenting and determined. Koko lay near her straw-bed and chewed on a stick, unconcerned. Bandit stood over and behind her, trying to get it right, being driven by forces beyond his control. She just wouldn't cooperate! For his own good, I made Bandit come inside, which did not please him, and he barked persistently to be let back out. The next day on our way back from the river, he collapsed altogether as we crossed the parkway. I was completely alarmed, but as it turned out, he was just totally exhausted from the day before. Koko and I jogged on ahead to get the car. Bandit and Daniel waited for us under a tree.

Monday came. Koko had been sleeping outside now at night (by default), but I had made her stay in the night before, so I could be sure of catching her in the morning, when it was time to go to the doctor. Daniel had left on Saturday, so I was on my own. She knew right away something was up, and resisted with all her might as I dragged her to the car and loaded her into the backseat. Bandit looked on.

We arrived at the clinic and I pulled up in back, as the plan went. I left Koko in the car and ran in to tell them I was there. Then I went out to join Koko in the backseat. The doctor came out and administered a mild sedative and muscle relaxant to her. He said it would take a little time for the drugs to act, and asked if I would be okay. I assured him that I would. He left us there and went back inside. The temperature was in the 'teens, and though it was a little cold, I was used to being out in the elements, and in temperatures much worse than this. My hands had never been in such terrible shape. They were dry and cracked from the repeated exposure, and seemed to have turned permanently red. Dr. Goodman came out once, to make sure we were okay. He decided it needed a little more time to work. I stroked Koko's head in my lap as the drugs took effect.

The next time the doctor came out, he reached into the backseat and scooped her up. Her eyes screamed in terror, but her body couldn't respond. He was used to my apprehension, and assured me, everything would be fine and that they would call me when she was done. Then they disappeared through the back door. The car felt noticeably empty. I climbed into the front seat and drove home. The yard felt empty too. It was funny, how quickly she had made a place in our lives. Bandit was mildly impressed that Koko was absent when I returned; perhaps he thought she had finally gone home. He curled up in his straw, contentedly.

I tried to get involved in something around the house, but I was preoccupied. Finally the call came: Koko was ready to come home. I wasn't sure what condition she would be in, and I hoped I could get her home safely, if she was still groggy. But she was wide awake and alert. It took me a while to coax her out of the cage they had her in, and finally, I just had to drag her out. And then, to drag her out of the building. But she went into the car willingly, grateful to me for rescuing her. (She must have forgotten that it was me who had brought her there to begin with, which was good.) The doctor had done an excellent job. She was in good condition, in fact, it was hard to tell that she had just been through an operation.

Bandit sniffed her briefly when she got home, and immediately sensed the change. Never again would he show the interest in her, that he had shown over the previous weekend. Whatever she had that he wanted was gone. I can count on one hand, the number of times since, that he acknowledged her at all. But that was their relationship, and it worked for them.

Koko went immediately to her cave. I didn't like to see her down there, in the dark and dirty damp basement, so soon after her surgery. I put her on a leash and made her come upstairs. I had her lie down by the mattress in the bedroom, on the rug I had put there, especially for her. I had asked Clarrise to come by and baby-sit, while I took Bandit for his afternoon walk. Koko had never been alone in the house; and I knew how she reacted, when she was locked in the basement. I assumed her condition was much more fragile than it probably was, and didn't want to leave her alone.

Clarrise came by and Bandit and I got ready to head out. Koko must have known we were leaving, by the tone of Bandit's bark, but kept herself stuck in the corner in the bedroom. I think Clarrise's presence might have had her on edge. I tried to tell Clarrise to leave her alone. If she pokes her head out, into the living room, I told her, just make like you're standing up, and I know she'll scoot right back into the bedroom. Koko had been through enough today already, and I thought Clarrise could respect and appreciate that. But of course, she didn't.

When I returned, Clarrise was lying across the bed, right in Koko's face; she had her cornered. I was dismayed, but again, held my tongue. Koko stared blankly ahead. I reached over and petted and soothed her. Clarrise had a couple of dog-bones in her pocket, which she brought out. She placed them between Koko's front paws, under her nose. Koko wasn't interested.

"Don't you want the bones?" Clarrise said, in her high-pitched, teasing voice. "Okay then, I'll just take them back!" she said, and reached out for the bones. As fast as lightning, Koko let go a warning yap, and snapped at Clarrise's hand. All right, Koko! I thought, and applauded her in my mind. It was the first time she had exercised any control. Clarrise recoiled, and chuckled nervously. "Well," she said, "I guess maybe she does want the bones, after all!" Clarrise also decided that it was a good sign, that Koko had shown some assertiveness. Finally, I got us out of the bedroom. It was after that incident that I decided, Clarrise would baby-sit no more, forever.

She wanted so badly to get her hands on Koko, but I could never figure out why. She was very seductive and insidious in her attempts, and I started to wonder if maybe she was some kind of a witch, or sorceress, as she had prescribed various herbal remedies and "natural" solutions for Koko's maladies and nervousness; also, she had often brought some strange and unusual recipes over to the house, for us to try. I wondered what her motives were, and what kind of an unwitting pawn she wanted Koko to be. The only other person who ever checked up on us, who floated in and out of our lives occasionally, was Maryanne and Zack, from the river days. As it turned out, they only lived a couple of blocks west of us. But Koko liked Zack, and Maryanne was totally unpretentious. I began to think of her as the benevolent factor in the equation. It was something to do with good and evil, and crows, and innocence, and supreme forces, that somehow I had stumbled into the middle of.

XXIX.
Johnny Quest

It was a Sunday morning. I was up early as usual. The house was quiet. I was looking forward to watching "The Adventures of Johnny Quest" at six-thirty, as it had become my habit to do, since Koko's arrival. I settled into the tender morning with a fresh cup of coffee, to watch the show. It was an episode I hadn't seen before. The adventure took place in a jungle environment. Hadji and Johnny were on the scene, as was Bandit (the cartoon dog). There was a little, brown spider monkey too, swinging on a vine, teasing and provoking the ever perplexed Bandit. I watched with half a mind, as my thoughts turned to the tasks for the day. Suddenly my attention was caught, as I heard Johnny say, "Hey! Bandit! That Coco is really giving you a run for your money!" (The particular spelling is my own.) The monkey's name was Coco!

And for that enlightened moment I was stranded in time. The house was dark and the world was silent, offering no regard. Then it all became clear: none of it had been in my control! It had all been preordained! (But for what purpose? I still ask.) Then I snapped back to the moment, and realized, it was just a strange coincidence. And we laughed about it, and cast ourselves in the roles, with Clarrise as Dr. Quest (though eventually we would think she was really the evil Dr. Zin, *posing* as Dr. Quest.) Yes, it was a very strange coincidence indeed. Especially since the characters of the two animals, so closely resembled that of their live counterparts. Bandit was forever forward and serious-minded; Coco was ever playful and mischievous. And Koko did like to play.

She was constantly pestering Bandit, trying to provoke him to play. But he had no interest in that at all, and would only grumble at her and escape inside his house. But it didn't take long for her to learn, that if she could get Bandit to squawking, I would come out of the house. Then she would flick her tail at me and run behind the big tree, trying to entice me to play. And I would. I would give mock chase, and off she would run, ducking and dodging, hurling and whirling around the yard, but cautious she was in her abandon. If the game got too intense, her tail would droop down and she would start looking at me sideways. Then I knew it was time to back off. I let her set the limits, as we tested each other.

And it was through this play, that we first began to establish a bond; and a camaraderie developed. We used the big thick rope, from the river days, to engage in lively games of tug-of-war. She was familiar with this game, and already knew how to play. And by playing, I was able to gradually bring her closer and closer to me, until I could have reached out and touched her. But I didn't, for that would have spoiled the game. Over the weeks, I watched the expression in her eyes go from meek compliance, to cautious defiance. I encouraged her, all the way. And as we played, I began to make brief eye contact with her. Initially, it would send her scurrying off, but eventually, she could stand it a little. I was always careful to avert my eyes first: I didn't want to dominate her, I just wanted to make contact. One day, she would come to know my eyes and each expression, as I would know hers, and even look to them for direction, but that would be a long time coming. For now, we played deliberately and with restraint.

Koko was always at her most natural and precocious when she was left to her own devices, thinking she was unobserved, in the backyard. She always knew if you were watching her through the kitchen window, and she would become noticeably more inhibited and nervous. So I would go upstairs and watch from there. The window at the top of the stairs provided a perfect bird's-eye view to the backyard; and from there, I would peek into her world.

She had more fun, all by herself, than one could imagine (though she constantly checked for Bandit's presence, and expected him to be there, posted in his triangle). She already had a pile of "stuff" collected by her bed of straw, for her diversion. There was an old broom, with most of the straw pulled out and the handle chewed on; the dog-bowl we had purchased, especially for her, that didn't look much like a bowl anymore; a few plastic gallon milk-jugs, shredded and in pieces; a tennis ball with no sheathing, the inside of a softball, socks with no mates, a couple of leashes with no hooks, and numerous other dispatches of hers.

She would choose her plaything carefully from the pile. Then she would attack. She would rip it and shred it and toss it and retrieve it. She would pounce on it, and then holding it between her front paws, roll onto her back with it. She would hold the object of her affection high in the air, above her gaping jaws, then drop it directly into her waiting mouth. She would catch it and squirm from side to side. Then she would take it again in her paws, and lift it high, and drop it again, into her waiting jaws. She was a joke, and I couldn't help but laugh out loud. Then, all of a sudden, she would be up on all fours, standing as still as a statue: something outside the fence had caught her attention.

Her nose would go up to the breeze. Then she would start prancing around the yard, trying to hone in on the scent, her tail flying behind her like a flag. She was magnificent! She was strong and agile and a sight to behold. It was a side of her I had never seen before, but had always suspected was there. When she tired of all her other diversions, or when she just wanted to start a ruckus, she would turn to Bandit. This would become a major sticking point between Daniel and me.

Koko could be unrelenting. She would come at Bandit with her tail tucked down and her head lowered. She would drop her big paw on his head and drag it down. He would turn his head, this way and that, trying to escape her onslaught, but to no avail. (He had a slow time, getting up.) She would crawl to him on her belly. Then she would start with the kisses, and lick around and in his mouth, whimpering and whining, with the intensity building, until it appeared she might crawl right down his throat. He would growl and snap at her, with his lips in a snarl, and their canines, just a breath of air away from each other, locked in some kind of ritualistic performance. At first I took offense at the behavior, and thought Bandit's growling and snarling was purely a defensive reaction, and that he was truly distressed. But as it played out, I realized that Koko was just expressing her total servitude and submission to him, and what I perceived as displeasure on his part, was just his natural and ordained response. And the scene would play out over and over, sometimes several times a day. And Koko did have a tendency to overdo it, and then I would have to physically, drag her away from him. But she learned to respect his age and his status, and learned how to impose herself upon him, more gently. Then it was hilarious to watch, as she grew to be more than twice his size, to see her groveling before him.

But Daniel didn't understand at all. He was convinced she was "just being mean," and that she was going to hurt him, and eventually "she was going to kill him," by causing some irreparable injury. And then just to goad me, he would threaten to return her to the river. But I wouldn't buy into it, because I knew as well as he, that it was an idle threat, and that it would only happen over my dead body. And sometimes, I was worried too, that she might go too far, and accidentally hurt him. So as much as I could, I tried to stay on top of the situation.

I only resorted to a physical reprimand once with Koko; and I vowed never to do it again. She had been at Bandit relentlessly. I couldn't get her to leave him alone. She was in a frenzy, spinning and nipping and whining and licking at him. As she raced by me for the umpteenth time, taking another jab at Bandit as she passed, I heard Daniel's voice ringing in my head, she's gonna kill him! she's gonna kill him!, and almost by reflex, my hand came out and I swatted her on the rump. "No, Koko!" I said. Well, my hand slapped her on the rump a lot harder than I had intended it to, so much that my fingers stung, and immediately, I regretted it. Koko cringed and slunk away. Eyes that were full of play, turned to terror. She looked up and over her shoulder accusingly toward the sky, unsure of from where exactly, the blow had come.

"Oh, Koko, honey," I said, "what happened?" I was hardly able to admit, even to myself, what a terrible thing I had just done. Oh, I was sorry. I felt like such a brute. But she let me comfort her, briefly. To this day, I am so grateful that she never realized the blow had actually come from me. Never again, I vowed then, never again will I raise my hand to this creature. It was an inexcusable thing to do.

The days melted into weeks, and the weeks melted into Spring. Though usually I watched meticulously for every sign of its arrival, that spring, I barely saw it come. Koko slept outside most of the time now, and because the weather was more hospitable, so did Bandit. Koko could still be very evasive, but she would approach me in the yard, if I was lavishing my attention on Bandit. She would stand aloof, but just within arm's reach, and I would stroke her chest, with the tips of my fingers barely touching her fur. She wanted to like it.

And when my focus was expressly on Koko, Daniel would remind me not to forget Bandit, whose affect he was certain, was scowling and jealous. But though Bandit did go through a period of adjustment (as we all did), I believed we had an understanding, and it was Daniel who resented the amount of time I was spending with the animal, more than Bandit. I tried to explain to Daniel, that the time I was investing was necessary, and it would eventually pay off. Do you want a wild animal running around the backyard, I would ask him, or an animal that at least borders on civility? And he was always looking to blame Koko for something; and I always had a ready excuse. Sometimes it seemed as if he was deliberately trying to undermine my efforts.

One day, while we were at Dowling, when I was still letting Koko loose, there was a terrible collision. Bandit was up ahead in the orchard; we were still back by the gate. I let Koko go and she flew off across the field, directly toward Bandit. Just as she whizzed by him, at exactly the wrong time (a typical Bandit maneuver) he turned, and Koko nailed him. He went flying, and got up with a noticeable limp in his right, front leg. My heart was in my throat as I ran to him. Daniel had just the ammunition he needed. "I told you so! I told you so!" he said, and took Bandit from me and stomped off across the field with him, as if I could no longer be trusted with his welfare. I rounded up Koko, and we just stood there, abandoned. I felt like I was on a tightrope, with a fire burning at both ends.

Toward the end of March, Koko entered her "Chicken Little" phase. She ran crouching around the backyard, with her tail between her legs, looking up into the treetops, as if the sky was falling. We looked up too, just to humor her, but there was nothing to see. This went on for days into over a week. When it just got to be too much for her, she would retreat to her cave, to rest and relax. And when she came out again, the behavior would continue. One day, on top of all that, firecrackers began exploding in the next block. That did it! Koko ran to the front-most section of the fence, where she secluded herself when she was in the yard, and jumped. Her front legs were hung over the fence and her back ones were ready to follow. For a second she hung there, in a moment of indecision. But she decided against it, and dropped back down into the yard. I offered her the back door open, and she hurried to her cave. Then I knew for sure, Koko was home. And one day, as quickly as the chicken-little behavior had started, it ceased, and to this day, it still remains a mystery, exactly what she saw up there in the clouds.

After that, Koko entered her Gladys Kravitz stage. (She was the nosy neighbor who lived next to Darwood and Samantha, on "Bewitched".) Koko had to know everything that was going on in the neighborhood at all times. She watched the neighbors intently as they did their spring yard work, and would rush "to see" if a car pulled up in front. She kept abreast of all comings and goings. Nobody walked by the house, unobserved. She would stand staring so intently at the intruder, but if they happened to even glance in her direction, she would scurry off, and hide behind the tree; or if she was in the house, she would peek out from behind the curtains. You could always read her reaction to a situation by watching her tail.

Koko's tail, once you learned how to read it, was a real barometer of her mood. It could go from flipped up and over her back, when she was especially aroused or excited, to plastered firmly between her legs, so far sometimes that the tip of it touched her chest in the front, when she was fearful or nervous. And there were varying degrees in-between. Her body language, once you learned it, was unmistakable. When she was surveying something with purpose, she would stand with her front legs spread out, and her head bobbing up and down on her long neck between them (which only exaggerated the hump of her shoulder blades), and with sheer intensity, scrutinize the offender. She was often in this posture, as we waited, stalled out on the sidewalk, for the traffic to clear at the four-way stop.

Koko would watch the passing cars, to make sure they kept moving, and no one exited the vehicle. Often, she would catch the casual glance of a person in the car, and for a frozen moment, their eyes would lock. Then Koko would start. And the person in the vehicle would drive away, besieged by visions of things wild I'm sure, to ponder the experience of being scrutinized by such timeless eyes—eyes that seemed to look right into your soul. And sometimes, I noticed a flash of fear cross their brow; for people are often afraid and taken aback by things wild, though it be the most natural thing on Earth. And for as many times as I heard the comment about Bandit, what a beautiful dog!, I would get questions about Koko. They were a daunting couple, and worth a look, although Koko abhorred the attention, and wished to be invisible. But she looked so out of place and out-of-sync, people couldn't help but stare.

XXX.
Our Door Is Always Open

Koko rarely came in the house. It was all just too strange. I would stand in the doorway and hold the door open for her, while she decided if she wanted to risk it. She would step one foot on the threshold, then pause. She would look up and from side to side. Then she would step back out. She would go and turn a complete circle and come at it again. She would poke one foot in the door, over the threshold, and touch the landing tentatively with her paw, as if she was testing the bath water. She would look up, and study above, poking her head in and out, as if trying to understand where the sky went. She just didn't know about this big box-like thing we humans called a house. And then, not only would she lose the sky, but she would have to pass close by me, to make her way in. She knew I would close the door behind her, and then she would be trapped. Finally, my patience would run out, and I would simply prop the door open. And as I moved away and went further into the house, she would come along behind. But she was very mindful, not to let anybody get between her and the door, and if you headed in that direction, she would run out ahead of you. So for the most part, at least during the waking hours (and sometimes during the night), the door was just left open. And when she did dare to venture into the house, she was aghast at the things she saw.

She didn't know what to think of the television. The voices and sounds that came from it took her aback. She approached it cautiously, looking all around it and checking behind it, to see where the voices were coming from, always ready to flee. She was sure that it was some kind of a trick, and someone was going to pop out at any minute, to try and take a hold of her. She would eventually get used to the dull and constant drone of the set. The stereo bothered her less, though she did have particular tastes. She didn't mind James Taylor, or even Neil Young, and she cocked her head at the strange noises that came off of Paul Simon's *Graceland*, but Dylan (and I hate to say it) would always send her out of the room, especially when he started blowing on the harp. I think she just had very sensitive ears.

One night, I was awakened to the sound of Koko banging on the door. She was asking to be let in! It was about two o'clock in the morning, and this was a first. I leapt to answer, but it would not be that easy. It was time to play the door-game.

Koko wanted to come in, but could not make herself go by me. It was the one-foot-in, one-foot-out routine. It was only April and the nights were still very cold. I stood there as long as I could, but was losing my patience. She wouldn't come in, so I closed the door and went back to bed. In minutes, she was banging on the door again. I got up and went to answer. Still, she would not pass by me. Finally, I propped the door open and backed away, around the corner in the kitchen. I could see her reflection in the microwave, and waited for her to come in. Finally, she did. She ducked way down low, looked this way and that, then scooted down to her cave. I waited a second or two, then went behind her and closed the door. Of course, by that time, Bandit had taken full advantage of the open door and had escaped outside to post himself stubbornly in his straw. I let him stay there; for though it was chilly out for me, it was pleasant enough for him.

But Koko had not come in to sleep, she was up to some mischief. I could hear her rustling around in the front room. I heard her go up and down the basement stairs. When I heard her in the living room again, I thought I had better go and investigate: no telling what she was up to. When she heard me get up, she headed for the basement. I never actually saw her (the house was quite dark), but I could hear her nails clicking on the tile, and then her clamoring down the stairs. She had several things pulled out of the bookcase in the very front room. Nothing of any real importance was damaged. A few plastic gizmos, with identifiable teeth marks in them, and some old bank statements were lying on the floor. My friend Margaret (who by that time was in the hospital), had given me some money to hold for her, in case she needed some incidentals, during her convalescing. I had put the envelope with the one-hundred dollars in it on the top shelf of the bookcase, alongside some old cassettes. I reached to find it, but it was gone! I looked around and didn't see it on the floor; I headed down the stairs after Koko. She peeked out at me from behind the furnace. I looked to my right, and there, lying on the floor right outside her cave was the envelope, torn to bits. And right beside that were the five, twenty-dollar bills that had been inside it, all lying neatly in a row, as if they had been laid there by someone's hand. I looked at Koko. "You're damn lucky!" I told her, and I could tell by her expression, that she thought so too.

So we began to Koko-ize the house. We divided things into two categories: expendable and non-expendable items. Though Koko never went about to be totally destructive and ransack the house, she did have her peculiarities. Most of the items she showed an interest in were things I had handled recently, or things that had come in from another house. (I had to be very careful when I borrowed books from people, lest she take an interest in them.) It was amazing, how many really non-essential items we had. Once she got a hold of something, and it was itself no more, there was always a reason why it had been expendable: it never did work right, the handle was broke, the light didn't come on, etc., and it got to the point where we all but thanked her, for relieving us of that useless item. If something was missing, Koko was suspect. And costly mistakes were made, until we learned to keep what we valued out of her reach.

And she would watch for mistakes. She would stroll through the house taking inventory. I could almost see her making a mental list of what interested her, that she would be back to examine later, in further detail. She was hard to discipline. She took it so to heart, and the betrayed look in her eyes caused a pang of guilt that made you regret ever scolding her. Then she would flee to her cave, to hide and sulk, and she would look at you suspiciously for the rest of the day, and maybe even into the next, and into the next. No, it just wasn't worth it. Basically, she got away with murder.

That spring, we took down the waferboard fence and put up something a little more pleasing to the eye. I raised the pickets on the back gate, which we were using again. We used lattice panels and two-by-fours to raise the fence. We did the same thing in the front, adding a little "garden gate" so we could gain access to the side yard. Eventually, all the flowers that lived in the backyard were moved to the flower-beds on the side of the house, as Koko decided her job was to nip off every bud, before it could blossom. And this irked Daniel to no end. But Koko loved to provoke, and Daniel's irritation only made her more intent on destroying the foliage, and they were in constant battle over it all summer. Koko would deliberately stand amidst the flowers, and watch closely, Daniel's reaction, as she nipped the bud off the nearest plant. Then she would stand there, with the purple or red or yellow petals hanging out of her mouth and lying around her feet, and wait for his reply. The more he scolded her, the more determined she was to do it and she made a real game of it. Then Daniel would call for me, and tattle on her, and expect *me* to take some kind of action. But I was not willing to alienate her over some simple and silly plants, and he chided me, for my lack of discipline. I had decided that there was only so much you could do, and she took such delight in her naughtiness, she was hard to deny.

One day she decided that the tv cable, that ran down the outside of the house in the back, was a fun thing to pull on, and she was determined to release it from whatever was holding it inside. I caught up to her on that one, but then she discovered the telephone line, on the other side of the house, and we nearly had our service interrupted. The more you scolded her and took notice, the more determined she was in her task. Eventually, we put metal sheathing over the outside wires, and that deterred her (although our television reception has never been quite the same). And she did sever the phone-line in the house one time, but that was by accident. It had been lying so close to the chew-toy she had been working on so diligently, and she just got confused. And that was easily replaced. But it made me look around at the jumble of wires on the floor, that connected my speakers and microphone and my guitar to the mixer, and I decided that my music would definitely have to be moved upstairs. And as it turned out, it was a change for the better. It was the perfect seclusion: *my* cave.

Being at that age, Koko loved to chew and did so incessantly. She would chew the boots right off your feet, if you sat still long enough. We used up everything we had, and soon found ourselves begging for old shoes from our friends. And she loved to hear things rip and tear. It was like music to her ears, and the sound of it would excite her all the more. We doled out an old ten-by-ten foot carpet to her, piece by piece, until she eventually ripped and shredded the entire thing (making it much easier to discard). And as she grew, so grew her teeth, until she earned the nickname, Jaws. And she was like a surgeon with them. She could pick apart the smallest detail, with her incisors, or snap a branch like nothing, between her big bone-crushers, in the back. She wasn't shy about giving you a good nip, especially once your back was turned, and you had to be on your guard. And she was fast. She would whiz by you, and at her discretion, grab a slight hold of your pants, give you a gentle nudge with her nose, or give you a quick pinch with her teeth, which would eventually turn into a little black-and-blue mark: a "kiss" from Koko. It was a dangerous game that we played, but she played it with precision, and though there were plenty of opportunities for a lapse in judgment on her part, she never amputated a finger, or other important body part. When it came to Koko, her bite was definitely worse than her bark. Up until now, she hadn't said a word.

And when she did, it was a tremendous, earth-rendering sound (I think she might have even surprised herself). One day, it came booming out of the backyard. Koko had a voice! And what a voice it was. It was loud and sharp, but she used it sparingly. And then there was the deep, low, throaty bark, that meant a person was encroaching. And eventually, I would come to understand all of her noises, her whimpers, and squeaks, and whines and barks, and I knew what each one meant; whether a dog was passing by, or a stranger was at the door or someone was too close to the fence. And though she looked ferocious enough, when the threat was on the outside, I wondered just how she would react if the threat came inside. But with the way she looked when she was all riled up, hunched up, with her hackles raised and her teeth bared (like some kind of huge, mutant raccoon), only the foolhardy would try.

I began to try to teach Koko some basic commands. I used special treats for an incentive. She was very wary of me, and first I had to get a hold of her. And then she looked at me fearfully, as I pushed her butt to the floor, and told her to sit. But having done that once, and with the promise of a treat, she did it by herself, on the very second try. She was extremely keen, and picked up easily on voice-tone and words. And she would sit when I told her to, usually, but she would always sit at a distance, just out of arm's reach.

The next command she needed to learn was to stay. That way, I could get a hold of her when I needed to—I thought. But this command would always be followed only at her discretion. I would tell her to sit, and then stay. If she allowed me to reach out and touch her, I would give her a treat. If she dodged me or bolted, no treat. I was rewarding her for allowing me contact. And it worked, but very sporadically. When she really didn't want to be caught, you could neither bribe nor trick her. And the harder you tried, the more suspicious she became, until it was hopelessly impossible.

The next thing she needed to learn, was to come. That was an especially hard one for her, because it went against every instinct she owned. I would put her on a long lead at Dowling, and reel her in, as I repeated the command. And eventually she learned what was expected, but what she did with that knowledge was again, up to her own discretion. Bandit had always had trouble with that one too, and when she watched his response to the command, as he completely ignored me, or turned and went in the total opposite direction, I shuddered to think what she was learning. She was set a very poor example, as to the parameters of the command "come." And I would explain to her that Bandit was being a *very* bad dog, and that she should pay him no mind.

Shaking-hands was a tough one for her too, because it meant actual physical contact, but it was a requisite. With her, the command became "gimme four," and she would reach out and slap your open palm with her paw. Then she would sit there preciously, and wait for her treat. Eventually she learned the "down" command too, and would repeat all of the basic four, in rapid succession, if she thought a treat was forthcoming. She certainly had an irresistible way about her.

Summer allowed me to spend more time in the yard with the dogs. We were really getting to know each other. And though sometimes I still looked strange to her, she often looked very strange to me as I exited the house in the morning. She would come up to me with her ears laid back, swinging her butt back and forth (though still not to touch), and with her face looking so long and narrow, and the markings on it, so dramatic, and by the deep yellow hue in the back of her eyes when they glowed in the sun, I was sometimes taken aback, and made to wonder how this strange creature had stolen into our lives.

I loved her so much, I could hardly imagine life without her now. She had established herself so firmly in our lives, and had become an intricate part. She was often aloof and difficult to manage, and her ways sometimes were hard to figure, but figure them I did. I could tell by the expression in her eyes what she was thinking. The position of her tail and the way of her stance spoke a language to me, that told of her mood and persuasion. I knew Bandit by heart, and now I was learning her. I knew just which words and gestures would bring her close, and what would drive her away. And she began to know me. And we played that summer, and wrestled and chased, and she pranced around the yard, and took her shots at me, and I took mine at her, and we learned a lot. But no one ever saw her in this form, except me. And my friends probably wondered at my obsession and fascination with this strange animal, who fled to the basement whenever they arrived. And the only evidence I had of her, were the pictures that hung on the refrigerator. But to me, she was a treasure, though a hidden one, she was.

Winter arrived again inevitably, and it was only by the weather, we were kept apart—and by the Furnace Monster. Koko hardly came in at all. I would go out and sit with the dogs, on the sunny side of the yard, in the big bed of straw that was amassing, for as long as I could stand it, but I was only human. Rather, I would have shuttered myself inside. And with the diminished human contact, and the long, silent winter nights, Koko would go a little wild. (Winter would always be her "wild" season.) But when she got too lonely (because Bandit was in at night) or if she just wanted to gain some attention, she would bang on the door to come in. And then it would be a repeat of the first winter before, and we would play the door-game out, to its conclusion. I would be up several times during the night: it was impossible to sleep, with her trouncing across the bed to go out, every time the furnace fired; and it was impossible to sleep with her outside, banging on the door to come in. That spring, as soon as the weather lifted, we put in a doggie-door. And that is what made all the difference.

XXXI.
The Turning Point

Now Koko could come and go as she pleased. It didn't take long for her to learn how to use it, and she loved the freedom the door provided (and I started to sleep through the night). But Bandit would never use the doggie-door (I suspected he wouldn't), and that was good. Because I could just picture him coming through the door, with Koko in hot pursuit, and him flying down the basement stairs. He preferred just to stand at the door and bark, and wait for someone to come and attend to him. And now, I didn't have to worry about leaving her in the yard either, for she always had access to her cave, which was her ultimate, safe place.

She went there to escape the heat of the summer, and the noisy activity that pervaded the neighborhood. And sometimes I would go to her there, just to sit and be with her. She accepted that and expected it. I would talk to her and pet her, and she would relax, and let me scratch her belly. It was a time for us to be quietly together, without any distractions, to re-establish our bond; and it renewed something in me, to be with her.

Clarrise came by occasionally, sometimes bringing a dog or two along, but Koko wasn't so interested in playing with them anymore. She was more concerned with the stash of dog-bones she had hidden around the yard, in various locations, and monitored closely, the movements of her canine visitors. If one happened to wander too close to one of her stashes, she would let them know, in no uncertain terms, that this was her terrain; hers and Bandit's, for she always yielded to him.

Now with the doggie-door, Koko moved like a phantom through the house: the door barely made a sound as it swung open and closed. She could appear in a moment and be gone just the same, and it was rather unnerving, the way she appeared and disappeared, literally in the blink of an eye. She was silent and undetectable. And we wondered how we ever got along without it. She came and went freely and you could never be sure, whether she was in or out. Sometimes, I would be sure she was asleep in her cave, and would be surprised to see her rise from the bedroom. Or I would swear she was outside, then would notice her passing silently behind me, as I worked in the kitchen. One night I woke up and she was lying beside me in bed, stretched out and snoring, as if it was the most natural thing to do; I didn't disturb her. When I woke up the next morning she was gone; and the occasion would never repeat itself. I guess she just wanted to see how it felt.

And Koko knew the sounds of food: the refrigerator door, the beeping sound the microwave made when the food was ready, the *chink!* of the fork on the dinner plate, and she would always rise to the occasion. She would stand in the kitchen and watch me twirl and whirl around as I prepared the meal (I used to be a short-order cook) and wait for it to be served. And she could never understand why we couldn't eat the *whole* roast beef, or the *whole* rotisserie chicken. And after a meal like that, whenever the refrigerator door opened, if you glanced toward the back door, you might see a nose peeking in the doggie-door, and one eyeball, staring at you hopefully. Then I would tell her, "You can come in!" (she always needed permission), and I would dole out a piece of the delectable dinner to her, just for being so adorable.

We celebrated Koko's second birthday that spring: we had tentatively set it at the Ides of March. And we celebrated the Rites of Spring, and cast our gloves to the Goddess of Destruction. (It had become an annual spring ritual, since Koko's main mission all winter had been to extricate the gloves from your hands. It made for a lively game, and was a welcome diversion for her during the long, cold winter months. And though you might have let a pair or two go in October or early November, by December you were hanging onto them for dear life. And if you gave them up to her too early, you would find yourslf at the store, searching frantically for another pair.) And our hearts rejoiced at the first sounds of spring: a basketball being dribbled down the sidewalk, yards being raked, and finally, the horns of the tow-boats on the river, such a lovely sound to hear. And the cardinals arrived, adding a dramatic splash of red, to the dim and faded landscape of the waning winter. And our lives settled into a decided routine.

Koko was again aghast at the people that emerged with the spring and absolutely refused to be led to the river. And though it was to my dismay (for I discovered, I longed to go there as much as Bandit), we relegated ourselves to the yard at Dowling. And Bandit learned to be content with that. He had turned thirteen that spring, and though he could still go the distance, sometimes he couldn't make it back. His mind still raced ahead, but his body was pressed to follow. Many of the limitations placed on us by Koko actually worked in his behalf. She refused to ride in the car, and though Bandit loved to go, he had a hard time entering and exiting the vehicle, and could no longer hold his own in the backseat; so it was really to his advantage, that we stayed out of the car.

I dutifully took Koko walking with us everyday, and she dutifully came along. I thought the more she went out, the more at ease she would become with the world, but it never happened. She was mostly just scared and nervous, and suspicious of every human form we encountered. She just couldn't get it through her head that I was not about to let anybody approach her. So we spent a lot of time at Dowling, hiding in the trees, and Daniel would look at us and say we were like two peas in a pod, although I'm not exactly sure what he meant by that. And once Bandit took care of his business, we would run home.

It took me over a year to realize that the animal just did not care to go for a walk. After dealing with Bandit's insistent wanderlust for so many years, it was a hard thing for me to grasp. So when it was walk-time, and she was being elusive and evasive, we would just leave without her. And although she didn't care to come, she didn't like being left behind either, and would jump and bark at the fence. But she was so laden with domesticity by that time (and an abundance of foods from the four food groups: chicken, beef, pork and chicken), I wasn't afraid that she might go over. And she had no place to go, except to find Bandit.

We used to say jokingingly, if enough people call you a wolf, you'd better start howling. Then one day, she did. It was the second Spring. Bandit and I were returning from our afternoon walk when I heard it. It was a long, drawn-out, strange and haunting sound, that came floating in on the breeze, whose octaves rose and fell, then faded to a soft warble. It was like nothing I had ever heard before! and it made something stir deep within me. And it brought to mind visions of the North Woods, marshes and forests and vacant fields. I stood captivated: the sound resonated in the pit of my stomach and tingled the hairs on the back of my neck. But I have yet to witness her, during her howling performance (although Daniel has described the scene to me, and the wind-up that takes place before the howl sets forth), because the only time she expressed herself this way, was when Bandit and I hit the trail without her. And I had a special signal for her, that was somewhere in-between a howl and a whistle, and when I heard her lonesome song, I would respond, to let her know that we were on the way. Then she would sit under the big maple tree and wait, and greet us as if we'd been gone forever. But Bandit heard none of it.

It was hard to determine just how bad Bandit's hearing had become, because he never did listen to me. But by that summer I was convinced he had lost it all. One day, as he lay on the rug in the dining room, the doorbell rang and he never budged. And that was the one thing that had always set him off in the past, guaranteed. Now it was Koko, who came charging into the house, through the doggie-door, to see who was there. (If it was company, and they entered the house, she would flee to her cave.) And when they were in the yard together, Koko was his ears. He would watch her reactions, and by them, tailor his response. Sometimes it was nothing, but a scent she had caught on the wind, and he would still bark, just in case, though at the empty air. They were becoming a team, and he came to rely on her, as much as she relied on him. I think she was a comfort to him, in his old age, though he would never admit it. They were Yin and Yang, Beavis and Butthead, Bonnie and Clyde, Sonny and Cher. And I had a part to play in it too, for I was their supreme commander.

We were again another thing, when we were a threesome. I immersed myself into their canine world that summer, a world ruled by scents and sounds and nips and growls. We played and joked and fought and loved. We lived in a secret world of our own design, and I was honored to be a part. Daniel drifted in and out, adding a fourth dimension to the plot, making waves where he could, as we became so established and complacent in our routine.

There was play-time for Koko in the morning and evening, and twice-a-day walks for Bandit. I finally accepted the fact that Koko would never be like a regular dog: she would never sit tied outside the corner store, while I went in for a gallon of milk, or wait patiently for me in the car, while I shopped for groceries. She was happy just to stay in the yard (although she was beginning to develop a keenness for her walk to Dowling in the morning, but *only* there, then *directly* home), and she seemed happiest of all, when we were all together. Yes, Koko was going to do what Koko was going to do. And if you couldn't work with her, you had to work around her: there was no fruit in going against her. The cost of that was fear and alienation. We were separate but inseparable. The only thing that kept us apart was the winter.

The State Fair came and went, and winter was upon us again. It came earlier than usual, and all of November was cold and ice. It was a rough time for Bandit, as even a few inches of snow could prove to be a major impediment, and I silently thanked the people who shoveled their walks, and especially those that shoveled through the snowbank to the street. Otherwise, I would scoop him up in my arms and carry him, over snowbanks and across icy walks, to a place where he could navigate more easily. Sometimes, he would slip and fall, and I would catch my breath and run to him, fearful that he was hurt, and help him up. But as soon as his feet hit the pavement, he was off again: he was unstoppable. And as winter arrived, so did the Furnace Monster, and Koko relegated herself to the out-of-doors. Because although we had fought many a fight, and won many battles, we could never beat the Furnace Monster. Koko was an enigma, and always would be.

XXXII.
The Final Verse

It is just past two years to the day since Koko came to stay with us, as I write this final verse. January is grueling and unrelenting as always; and we all ask ourselves why we live here, and count each cold day as one less to go through. And I harken back to those days on the hill, that fateful January, and wonder how we all survived it. Our history is now recorded in terms of "before" and "after" Koko, such an impact she has had on our lives. In some ways she is still unreachable, and sometimes still, untouchable. But when she does touch you, she touches you someplace deep and profound; her presence can overtake you.

She is a dichotomy of things and a paradox: she is flawed, yet flawless; she is brilliance and bafflement. She is ancient and new, she breathes delight and despair. She is the conqueror and the conquered; she is cowardly, yet brave. She is the Jester, the Imp, the *Provocateur*. She has caused me to feel such a range of emotions, and with a depth I never knew. She has brought me to tears, in both joy and sorrow. I have never smiled so deeply, right down to my soul, or laughed with such sheer delight. She is Joy. By her nature she is pure and without guile. I do not keep her, she chooses to stay. I do not own her, but together we are bound. Sometimes it is with her in all the world, that I feel most attuned. She has allowed me to reach that place inside, where the wind blows through the trees, and actions are guided, not by logic, but by instinct and desire. It is a place we all possess.

In some ways, Koko has been transformed, but in other ways, she has changed very little. She still likes to raid the house now and then, and only yesterday, I found my calculator out in the snow—the one I'd had for years. But it was old, and the decimal point was somehow stuck at two places, so good riddance to that! I say. She still hurries to the basement when certain people drop by, though there are certain ones she will tolerate, and there's even a couple she's happy to see (she's beginning to realize the significance of the pizza-delivery person). And she knows no caress, but Daniel's and mine, and in many ways, she is mine alone. When she does dare to venture into the house, she is careful not to let anyone get between her and the back door, so afraid she is of being "caught." (But we've already caught you, Koko! we tell her then.) And sometimes I look at her lying on the long, green couch (handed down to me by my mother), the same couch I used to lie on during my teen-age years (years I still look back on with a certain sense of bewilderment), and think how my life has changed since then, and how I never thought I would be here and now, and especially not with a wolf-creature on my couch. (And sometimes I can't help but wonder, why must *I* be her caretaker in this world, this stranger, this interloper? But one cannot argue fate.) And Koko still doesn't care to go anyplace except to Dowling, and that is good for Bandit.

Bandit will be fourteen this spring and it shows. He is often forgetful. He can be very demanding and is more stubborn and crotchety than ever; but I am patient. As his body grows feeble, so does his mind, and we chide him for his old-age symptoms, but it is all in good fun, for we know, we will all be there someday. And I yell at him a lot more, but it is just because I know he can't hear. And even though he can't hear, we are still not hastened to use the *w*-word, for it is taboo, and may only be spoken in hushed and darkened rooms. So I communicate with him by gesture, which Koko rarely picks up on, and I cue her by voice (which Bandit can't hear), so with each of them separately, I can be in collusion. And it is Koko who gets us rolling in the morning, with a certain set of signals and signs, that let Bandit know, it's time. And he still goes twice-a-day, though sometimes it's just around the block, and depending on the conditions, even that can be a chore. But as long as he is willing to go, I will take him. For it is his desire for "just one more time around the block" that keeps him going on.

He walks so slow now, it is hard to imagine him in his youth. Though he never waited for me, I find myself waiting for him. There is a slow and steady pace at which he goes, but I can tell by the way he looks at me over his shoulder, when he thinks he is "making a break for it," though his pace hardly quickens at all. And I am reminded of one of those simple wind-up toys: get the feet going, point him in any direction and off he goes. Block his path, he turns, and heads off in a new direction, never faltering in his step, forever forward. He didn't care where we went anymore, as long as we went. We could be a block from home, and for all he knew, we could have been in Scranton.

And it is hard to watch him grow old, with his heart of gold, and as big as a mountain, dreading the day to come, when it stops beating at all. And when I nuzzle in his fur, I try to register the scent of it to some memory cell in my mind, to call upon in the future, when I need him to be there with me. And I am afraid that when I lose Bandit, to some extent, I will also lose Koko. For when all is said and done, it is him she relies on. He is the tie that binds. And when he is gone, I will know for sure, how strong is the bond we forged. And then there will be more chapters to write, for without him, she will surely be lost, as we all will be. He is an integral part of her being, and her being in this world (and I fear that she will look for him forever, and that will doubly break my heart). And when he is gone, we will all sit together under the big maple tree, and sing a mournful song.

But for now, we are blessed with his good health, and we are a pack of four. Daniel is the roving member of the group: he goes out to forage, and we all share in the bounty. Sacrifices have been made, on all our parts, but they are made gladly. For truly, we are blessed. And sometimes we ask ourselves, why did *we* recieve this special gift? Why us? And why this time and in this place? But these are all eternal questions, and the answer lies somewhere between here and infinity. Maybe on my dying day, in a brilliant flash, I'll know. But for now, we can only cherish the gift that has been bestowed, and hold it in safe-keeping. And I hope that I have enriched her life as much as she has enriched mine. But when her eyes sparkle with glee, and her tail swings so wide, back and forth, that she hits herself in the eye with it, I am sure I have; and it is all the answer I need.

It was a long and arduous journey, from that place to this, and there is still a road to go. I tell the story mainly to relieve myself of it and to explain to my friends where I've been. But I can't explain exactly how it felt, on that wild and frozen night in the backyard, with the moon shining down out of an empty sky, and with the air so cold it hurt to breathe, as we stood together, this beast and I, with our senses strung tight to the wind, and for just one moment, our hearts beat as one.